SHADOW AND STONE

MELISSA WRIGHT

THE FREY SAGA

SHADOW and STONE

MELISSA WRIGHT

SHADOW and STONE

THEA

THEA HAD BEEN A SENTRY FOR EXACTLY ONE DAY WHEN SHE WAS thrown into the biggest conflict the North had seen in centuries. The dark elves had nearly gone to war with the fey, and Junnie, the new Council head, rode side by side with Thea and her childhood friend Steed, who had become one of Seven to the Lord of the North, as light and dark elves joined forces to overcome traps laid by the fey. Thea had stood upon the stones of the high fey court with her blade in hand and her life on the line. She'd been terrified but had felt no less than a warrior. Thea had found her calling.

She'd not seen a lick of action since.

She dropped the bucket of muck she'd been carrying with a muttered curse, glaring up the pathway to her superior's leather-clad back. He wasn't even the head of the guard. He was a subordinate to a subordinate of the head of the guard, and he'd been riding her like a stolen mare.

Thea ran the back of her hand across her forehead, unsurprised when it came away wet, not with sweat so much but with plenty of the black gunk they'd had her scraping off the base of the stable block. She didn't even rate high enough to tend the animals.

It wasn't as if she'd had lofty expectations. Before she'd left home, she'd heard all the criticisms: "You're too skinny. You're too young. You can't even wield a proper sword." They weren't all wrong. It was true she was thin, but she could hold her own. She wasn't much, but what there was of her was strong. And she was young, at least compared to those who'd warned her, but she was nearly as old as Steed, Grey, and the rest of the guard.

The sword wielding, though, she couldn't really defend. She glanced at her dirt-smeared hands, which were long and lean but scarred by the mistakes she'd made for the whole of her life.

Thea had worked with the animals in Camber, an occupation she'd loved. She'd been a healer, too, first for the animals, then the townspeople, and eventually for the occasional rogue. Word had gotten out, and she'd garnered a host of rogues, fighters, and ruffians as patients.

Her father had not approved. Thea had a bad habit of sticking herself in situations that didn't come out clean. It wasn't that she was clumsy, but she tended to go in headfirst—and in most unpleasant circumstances, feetfirst was the only good way. Her father used to tell her that it didn't hurt to turn tail and run once in a while.

She hadn't run, though. No matter how terrified Thea might be, she was always more afraid of running and of being called a coward than she was of fighting.

It was foolish, really, and immature, but there was no question that it had gotten her to where she was. And she had stood among legends, fighting beside the high guard to the

Lord of the North. Well, she hadn't done much fighting, but she'd stood with them.

She swiped her hands on the sides of her pants. "Done," she called up the pathway toward her superior's back.

He didn't acknowledge her. He was fool-headed and arrogant above his station, but Thea didn't tell him so. Instead, she trudged up the dark stone pathway to address him as he expected to be addressed. "Done," she said, "sir."

He glanced at her sidelong then back at the haze of a hidden horizon.

She waited. "Shall I—"

His glare cut her short.

She bit back her next retort.

"The blocks aren't clean," he said. "Start again."

Thea's mouth tightened for one long moment before she opened it again without regard for her better judgment. She was jerked to the side by a sudden pull on her arm, her curse heading for the source of the tug instead of her superior, but she drew up short. A stout black-haired boy in full leathers stared down at her.

"Thea," he said. "I've just finished my shift. Let me give you a hand."

He nodded at the guard, drawing Thea away from the man and back down the path. Thea had seen the boy before and had known him in Camber. Well, *known* was maybe a strong word. But she'd heard about him. Those dark eyes held a story as unhappy as any she'd ever been told. His name was Barris, and he was from a well-loved family—Thea's father and the entire town had thought highly of his parents.

They were gone now. His father, Burne, and his mother, Camren, had been killed in a single season when the new lord had fought for her throne. Thea wondered what made people give their lives for a person. For a cause, she could understand —for the North. But to lose so many for a single life…

Dreamer. Her father's word slammed into her, the way they often did when Thea lost sight of the present. She'd joined the cause, and she was present, even if it did mean sacrificing many to protect one. She would be cursed if they thought they could keep her from her aim.

Thea wrenched her arm free, picked up her steps, and leaned in so her narrowed gaze could target Barris's. "I don't *need* your help, you know."

Barris smirked. "Clearly. You were getting along well. Seemed like you were about to turn over a new leaf with your superior."

She rolled her eyes. "With the wall. I don't need your help with the *wall*." She kept her hands from flying, matron-style, to her hips. "You don't have to do my work for me."

"Oh, I'm not," he answered. "I just wanted to stop you from provoking our lead and getting our entire group thrown in a hole."

Thea stopped, making Barris glance over his shoulder to see her. "They don't do that," she said.

Her words were too timid, and she regretted them at once. Of course they didn't lock recruits in the ground as punishment—they wouldn't. Besides, the castle tunnels were just a legend. She'd not seen a single one.

Barris laughed. "No, they do not." He turned, crossing his arms over his broad chest. "But they do make you scrape muck off the stalls."

Her expression soured. "You're saying this is *my* fault? That idiotic, arrogant—"

Barris shook his head. "No, I'm sure you got sludge duty entirely without insulting your superior." He tossed her an empty bucket and looked at the pile of filthy rags, chisels, and short-handled spades. "Why are you doing this by hand?"

"Because it's virtuous," she spat. "Hard work is good for the spirit."

Barris stared at her. It was possible he was regretting stepping in to save her when she was clearly a loon.

She let her shoulders fall, defeated, then gestured with a tip of her head back up the path. "He made me."

Barris chuckled. "I see." He brushed his palms together, glancing surreptitiously to and fro. They were mostly alone there, out of sight of the other castle staff. "How about you keep watch, and I give you a hand. By the time he realizes you had help, we'll be enjoying mess."

Thea chewed her lip. She was hungry. And her superior *was* a big-headed idiot. "Whatever keeps you out of trouble," she said.

THEA DIDN'T REGRET LETTING Barris help. He'd worked quickly, and they were soon belly-up to the table, partaking in roast pig and crisp apples with the other castle guards. It wasn't her first time at mess, but she'd rarely made it on schedule, thanks to the extra tasks assigned to her by their lead.

The table was long with several benches, all filled with loud and chattering sentries and recruits, on either side. It might not have been her first time there, but it was the first time she'd not been exhausted and exasperated. It was the first time she'd actually enjoyed it. A few of the off-duty sentries laughed and told tales as dark-red wine sloshed in their mugs. The younger few, all new recruits, watched, laughing along but not joining in the drink, having quickly learned the rules were different for the seasoned men. Occasionally, Edan passed through the proceedings, but the head of the castle guard usually kept his distance during their off hours. It kept him from growing too close, inadvertently becoming a friend instead of the incontestable, or so the others had said. Edan was head of command, and his word was law. Only a high guard, one of Lord Freya's Seven, could overrule him.

Steed was one of the Seven. Thea plucked an apple stem from its core, annoyed that her thoughts had returned to Steed. It wasn't the first time she'd thought of him since she'd been stuck scrubbing palace walls. She knew it wasn't his responsibility to stick up for her or to point out to the other guards that she'd stood with them on fey lands. She didn't need him to win her a place among the guard. Besides, he might have thought she deserved her fate. Cleaning muck might be part of the process, an initiation.

She dropped two apples into her pocket as her eyes ran down the table to several dozen other guards. *They'd* not been cleaning stalls.

"Right." She tossed another apple into the air and caught it in a cupped palm before standing.

"Heading off?" Barris asked. He'd been leaning close to another guard, deep in conversation, but the seriousness seemed to melt from his face when he straightened to talk to her. Maybe she'd been imagining it. Maybe she'd been reflecting some invented torment of her own onto his face at the idea of losing either parent, let alone both.

"Yes," she told him. "Thanks for earlier."

Barris rolled his palm upward and gave her a smile that appeared entirely natural, not broken by grief or irrevocably scarred. "All in service to the guard." His brow shifted the slightest bit, his eyes sharing in his smile. "Stay out of trouble, aye?"

"Wouldn't think of it." She winked, tossing and catching the apple once more before she turned to go.

She was no longer hungry, not quite tired, and a day's ride from the haunts of her old home. Thea walked through the castle courtyards, still unfamiliar with the layout of the grounds. Edan had shown them the important paths, the battlements and balustrades and armories that pertained to their duties as guards. But Thea had yet to memorize the insignificant bits—nooks and crannies where one might be able to sit and hide, the smaller courtyards with leafy trees and garden shelves, and the overhangs that could keep one out of the rain. Thea loved a good hideaway, somewhere to stand outside of the bustle to watch the goings-on.

The castle had a lot of dark corners and more than its fair share of mysterious passages. She'd rarely been indoors for her duties those last weeks but would not have been surprised if the newly appointed castle staff got lost more than they found their way. It didn't help that Thea had practically lived out-of-doors before. When her parents had forced her inside, it had been into a four-room cabin, where she and her sister shared a single room. Cora had been the opposite of Thea in nearly every possible way. Growing up, Thea climbed trees and learned to shoot with a bow, while Cora sat indoors, sewing and singing and mixing perfumes for her hair.

"Wouldn't hurt you to wear a little perfume," she would tease Thea, her nose scrunched at some imagined outdoorsy smell.

Thea could always be counted on to return the favor, though, bringing in a speared fish or dumping a satchel of earth-covered mandrake root onto her sister's freshly prepared table. "Wouldn't hurt you to find a little food," she would say, parroting her sister's tone.

They'd grown up eventually, to their mother's great relief,

and Cora's hobbies had paid off. She had developed a talent—her embroidery and needlework were among the best in the land. Certainly, they'd surpassed anything in Camber. Cora had moved out of their small cabin last season, finally attaching herself to a trader their father had thought merely sold her wares. Thea's father had often been blind to the difference between Cora's business relations and those relations who were not, despite Cora's plunging necklines and red-painted lips. She'd been sly with more than just needlework, come to think of it, and had let Thea bear the brunt of her father's disapproval.

Cora had once had an eye for Steed when they were younger. She'd worked her magic with her soft, scented hair and blossom-pink cheeks. She'd even tied feathers and baubles into the two braided strands that crowned her dark curls. The attempt hadn't succeeded in the least. Back then, Steed had other things on his mind, such as the responsibilities his father had left behind, the horse trade, and a half-fey sister. Thea was surprised the boy had managed at all. But he'd had Grey. And he'd had that half-fey sister.

Given everything he'd been through, Steed had managed quite well.

Thea tossed her apple skyward as she ambled through an open stone archway. Maybe all the guards had some tragic history. It probably wasn't as bad as Barris's or Steed's, but the massacre had affected most of the families in the North in some way. Thea's family had been fortunate. Her father had kept them from getting involved.

She took a narrow stone corridor from one courtyard to the next and found herself once again on familiar ground. Low walls surrounded a large square of grass, the enclosure one of two where the horses could roam. Steed's stock there was limited, she'd heard. It had been discussed in town so many seasons ago, back when he joined the high guard. He couldn't bring them all in, so a few of the men from Camber had been put in charge of managing the remainder of the herds. The horses kept in the castle courtyards were lovely, the best of the best. She watched them graze, their coats slick and dark over thickly muscled frames.

Foot traffic had been walled off, and the atmosphere was quiet and peaceful and cool. The evening sun was fading, and a lone bird drifted across the darkening sky. Thea leapt onto the fence, hooking the heel of her boot over the stone to pull herself up. She landed in the grass on the other side, and a young gelding raised his head. Thea cooed, showing him the apple she held.

"There's a good boy," she told him, watching as he strode her way. "Someone's taught you about treats." She smiled when he nudged her with his head. She gave him a bite of apple, brushing her fingers over his neck. It was what she'd imagined when she'd come to serve as a guard. Thea had thought, foolish dreamer that her father had always said she was, that she could work in the stables, spending all day brushing and feeding horses.

It was ridiculous, her parents had said. And of course she'd known there would be battles, and of course, she'd realized she'd have to defend the castle on occasion. "Surely," she'd told them, "you don't believe they will stick a sword in my hand and throw me to the wolves."

Gooseflesh rose on Thea's arms at the word and the not-so-distant memory of the new light elves' Council head and her wolves. At first, Junnie had only moved the one of them, bringing it to the forest's edge to meet Thea and Steed. That had been disconcerting enough. But when they approached the fey lands, Thea had seen the truth of it and the power behind the light elf who had broken the old Council.

Freya had the same power, Thea understood, the ability to walk in the mind of a beast.

And in humans.

She shook off a chill, running a hand over the gelding's back. She walked forward, crossing the grass court, and pulled a second apple from her pocket. "Here's a pretty boy," she murmured, drawing another horse from his crop. The second horse bit into the apple, splitting it at the core with a snap that echoed through the courtyard. The sky had darkened further, but Thea sensed a shadow too dim to see. She glanced up as the bird circled lower and spread its massive wings. It was a hawk. The gelding nudged Thea, searching for the apple's other half. She laughed, gave it over, and rubbed between his ears.

"The stable yards are off limits," said a voice behind her.

She jumped, bumping the pair of horses on their heads as she turned. One of the geldings nickered.

"Steed."

He was too close. She'd not even heard him. Her heart hammered in her chest, and then she remembered he was her superior. She was on forbidden ground.

"I'm sorry," she told him. "I—" But she didn't have an excuse. She'd known where she was and wasn't allowed to go. Her shoulders fell. "What's my punishment?"

A gelding bumped her, knocking her arm out of the way to search for the last apple.

"You shouldn't treat them here," Steed told her. "No one wants to be headbutted every time they've got"—he gestured toward her side—"what is it you've got there?"

She held the small, ruddy fruit aloft. "Apple."

The gelding reached his long muzzle up and took it from her hand.

"That was the last one," Thea assured Steed.

"Good." He nodded. After a moment, he asked, "Is everything well?"

She shrugged. "It isn't exactly what I expected." He must have thought she was homesick, that she'd come to the horses because she'd missed it and wished she hadn't joined the guard. "I wouldn't change it," she added quickly. "Muck cleaning and all." She hated the way she raised her chin in defiance.

"Muck cleaning?" He chuckled. "So you've been getting on well with your lead."

Her posture, that challenge in her, immediately melted away. She'd deserved it, then. And Steed hadn't known. "They don't"—she cleared her throat to squash the emotion tightening it—"they don't report to you?"

He shook his head. "Chevelle oversees all that." Steed looked at her, his expression entirely solemn. "I've been asked to steer clear of the guard. Apparently, I've been a bit too approachable, and there's some concern that my natural affability might bring about some problems." He glanced over Thea's shoulder at the darkened arches that led to the stables. "Wouldn't do if I let slip someone breaking the rules."

"I see," Thea murmured. Steed had been reprimanded, and she'd put him in a spot. "And so"—she swallowed—"I should probably..."

Steed stared at her.

"...go?" she said.

Steed's brow lowered in a warning.

She bit her lip, trying to hide a smile. "I promise," she told him, but her words ran out, because the first rays of moonlight caught his eye, and she wasn't sure exactly what she'd meant to say. She would stay out of trouble—that would have been a good promise but one she couldn't keep. She would stay away from the horses—no, probably not. She would try. She could have said that. *I promise to try.*

She let out a breath that was nearly a laugh and ran past Steed to the wall. Her heart was alight with relief at narrowly escaping another rebuke, and she leapt to the top in a single bound. When her feet hit solid stone on the other side, she knew for certain that the castle was the only place she ever wanted to be.

2

RUBY

RUBY HAD EXHAUSTED HER SUPPLY OF HERBS AND OILS—WHAT was left of them after the fey had busted into her rooms and destroyed years' worth of stock, anyway—and still, Grey's wounds were tolerable at best.

"Quit fussing, Red," he said, leaning over a strap of leather he was stitching into some sort of weapons belt.

That was another thing the fey had destroyed, the best of their personal armor and weapons holders. She'd meant to replace Rhys's, specifically, as thanks for managing the hidden blade that had saved them both. She glanced over Grey's shoulder at the work then at his shirt, which sat in a wadded pile at his side. "Wait," she said. "Who are you making that for?"

He turned his chin to glance up at her.

His face was smooth and clean, not scarred like the rest of him from her enemies searing his flesh. They'd wanted her to see his face so she knew it was him. They'd wanted her angry.

He placed a hand over hers on his bare shoulder, and she resisted the urge to slip free of his touch. That was new, too,

13

her permitting Grey's easy touch and allowing him to be near her. He'd not pushed it. He'd known her long enough to take small steps, to give her space. Letting go of the distance she kept—not just from the man who cared for her but from all those she might have put into danger—was not the simplest of things. But she was trying.

She cleared her throat. "That's enough remedy for today, I suppose, at least until my delivery from Grenval's Peak comes through."

He let her hand go, not bothering to replace his shirt. Grey didn't mind the scars, and he certainly didn't mind the excuse to taunt her with his half-dressed nearness.

Ruby brushed a feral curl back into place then decided on a plait to occupy her hands. Her wild red mane had been a badge of heritage as she'd grown, a warning that she was part fey. It did not matter as much anymore. She was of the high guard, one of the Seven to Elfreda, Lord of the North.

"What are you plotting now?" Grey set aside the leather she suspected was for Rhys.

She frowned. "Nothing. I'll be a right proper guard and behave just as I've been ordered to."

He snorted.

She resisted the urge to smack the back of his head. Tucking the end of her last braid into the others, she added two small folded leaves from the ironwood tree. Ruby felt safer there than she'd ever felt in her life, but that was no reason to stop taking precautions. Pitt was still out there—she knew it.

Rumors after their battle on fey lands had spread faster than their own return to the castle. The fates had danced, the high fey lord's guard had betrayed him, and the changeling Pitt had tried to cheat the highest-held ceremony among the court. Veil's heliotropes had used their gift to take Veil's will, to freeze him in place while Pitt destroyed him. But the fey and Freya had come to Veil's defense. They had set right the ceremony in time for the high lord to be spared.

There had been an explosion of power. The keystones had been shattered to dust. And Pitt had disappeared.

The changelings had never given much regard to the court or their ceremonies, but Pitt had been especially indifferent. He'd had an agenda, a way to save himself from the blight the humans had brought to their lands. He'd stolen a potent ruby, stolen Ruby herself, and attempted a trade for her mother's diary, a document that told of magic and power and the means to keep him alive.

Pitt didn't care what happened to the other fey. He didn't intend to stop the humans from deadening the base power that was the lifeblood of his people. He simply meant to learn to harness it inside of himself in the way Ruby had been born doing, the way that came naturally to her because she was half elf. She didn't know if he could succeed, but he'd been clever enough to set into motion a plan from before she'd even come into being, so he was clever enough to escape with his life.

She wouldn't believe he was gone until she'd seen the husk of his corpse—no, not seen, because the changelings had the power to shift into other forms to fool the eye. She needed more. She needed to drive the dagger through his flesh with her own bare hands.

"Red." Grey pressed behind her to slide a palm over the fisted hand straining at her side. His voice was soft and low, his breath teasing her neck.

She sighed, letting Grey's touch ease her grip on the phantom blade. She would save the anger for later.

3

FREY

I CIRCLED SLOWLY OVER THE CASTLE GROUNDS, RELAXING INTO the mind of my best hawk and seeing through its eyes. The wind swept beneath the bird's wings, the air calmer and weather warmer as the season began to change. Beneath the bird and sky and beneath my own body where it waited in my rooms, everything had fallen into comfortable order. Gone was the chaos of the previous years, a time when another ruled and brought his people pain and strife. It was my place now, and conflicts were resolved by sense and law, not the whims of a man obsessed with power.

Granted, there were a few loose strings that needed tidying. We'd barely scraped by disaster with the fey, and as a result of my decisions, they were caged by ancient boundaries on one side and a small half-human girl on the other. No one had missed that I'd given Isa the duty of keeping the humans in check or that I'd nearly lost my throne in pursuit of my half-fey guard, Ruby. Taking on the fey and their problems was risk enough to our skin, let alone the shifting opinions of my people, given their distaste for halfbloods and my own heritage. But we had made it—we'd survived, and we'd gained the loyalty of Camber, the rogues, and most of the North. The realm was at peace.

My mother was gone, her memory finally laid to rest as the Council who destroyed her had been repaid the debt. And her aunt was head of a new Council, one I had hope for even if its people were not yet settled with the events that made it happen and the loss of so many of their own. I had my Seven, my Second, my home, and my birds.

Chevelle's soft breath hit my cheek, and I drew back from the mind of the hawk, peering out one eye to find him watching me.

"What are you smiling about?" he whispered.

I bit my lip, rolling toward him in the quiet dawn of our suite. "I'm happy. It's strange, isn't it?"

He traced a finger lightly over my cheek. "This is the way it should have been all along."

I kissed his palm then laced our hands together. "I don't think it will take me long to get used to it."

He grinned, leaning forward for a lengthy kiss. When he drew away, he looked regretful but not unhappy.

"Castle duties?" I asked.

He hummed agreement. "My lead is relentless."

I narrowed my gaze on him. "You'd better hope she doesn't hear you say that. I'm sure she could come up with more that needs tending."

He laughed, nipping my neck as he rolled past me to step off the bed. "Nothing would please me more."

I blushed, and it earned me a wicked flash in his gaze, but he backed away, knowing my delaying tactics well. I didn't try as hard as I might have—I had my own duties to attend. The kingdom had my days, but Chevelle had my nights. There would be time.

❧

WHEN I ARRIVED at Anvil's study, Rhys and Rider were well into their day's research, leaning over documents with a pile of discarded scrolls centered on the long table between them. They stood, because even if I kept forgetting, I was lord of this castle. I waved them down, but Rhys remained standing.

He inclined his head briefly before meeting my gaze again. "I thank you for the staff, Lord Freya. It is an honor that I will cherish."

I nodded, chagrined that I somehow had to express my emotions on the matter after I'd had Chevelle deliver a replacement for the one the fey had destroyed. "It is the least I could have done," I managed. "It is I who am grateful." I let my gaze fall to his brother, afraid to say more. The realm was settled, and I was at peace, but that didn't mean I could easily delve back into the turmoil that had nearly cost everyone I cared for their lives. Replacing a broken staff was the least of it. "How do you fare in your research?" I asked.

"Not much of interest as of yet," Rhys said. "There seems to be a lack of openly available information on the matter."

It was as I expected. Asher had been a hoarder of secrets, and even if his private vault was filled with documents, that didn't mean what we aimed to find would be easily secured. There was a variety of items on my research agenda, not the least of which were the methods the ancients used to secure the boundary between lands. We needed a more permanent solution because the wolves—ancients themselves in mind but not body—had to keep watch on the magic and methods, holding the boundary from breaking down, from all fey being able to cross at will into our lands.

The fey had found a way to use the humans who had brought them so much harm. There was a dampening about the humans, some *thing* that deadened the base magic running beneath the fey lands, and it was affecting the boundary magic as well. It had not been permanent at the boundary, but where the humans had encroached outside the fey forests, the base magic did not feel as if it could ever return. At some point, the humans would overrun that unknown threshold, and the power that gave the fey life would be gone.

I wasn't even certain the humans knew it. The elders had thought them low, so beneath regard that they were akin to animals. But I'd met a human, and I'd been inside their minds. They were not like animals.

"Rider," I said, thinking aloud. "There was a note in my mother's diary, something about the elders and their fear of humans." He nodded, and I did not elaborate—there was no need to explain that the note had referred to when the elders had found I was half human myself. "There was emphasis on a word I remember. 'Consume.'" Her harried script flashed in my mind, the emotion plain in her words. The elders had wanted to keep me from the others. They'd kept saying that she didn't understand.

They will consume you. The humans will consume us all, my mother had recounted. I shook off a chill, remembering her assessment and her shaky script near the end of the diary, written before the massacre of the North. *It is the want for power that will consume us.* She hadn't been wrong.

"I'll look into it." Rider scratched some note on a scrap of parchment.

"There is a legend in the ice lands," Rhys told me, "one of power lost and barren lands." I let my interest show, as I'd not heard much of the brothers' homeland and because barren ground seemed not unusual in the frozen realm from which they'd come. The ice lands did not host fey because the fey had to follow the vein of base magic beneath the earth. They could travel outside of their lands but not without cost. They needed to carry stones or risk forgoing access to their power while they were away. It was the lifeblood of their people. Those more powerful had less concern—the fey lord had ventured onto our lands without worry. Veil was powerful enough to be deadly even there, but with access to that untold energy, he was a force of nature.

Rhys leaned against the table, recalling the tale. "On the eastern reaches of a long-ago shore, before the water's rising ate away at the land, beings from beneath the waters would break the surface, heading over land in search of prey. They were long, dark water dragons with low, slithering bodies and spiked tails, and they fed on magical beings who strayed too near the shore."

I glanced at Rider, who listened nearly as intently as I. It sounded like one of Ruby's fey tales, and we all knew those were mostly true.

"One season, when the ice had melted far into the eastern plains, the creatures came in hordes. They poured out of the high waters, hungry for power in a way they'd never been. It is said there was a drought, that the magic had been stolen from its very core. And because of it, those creatures spread onto the ice lands, taking lesser creatures and elves alike."

"What happened?" I whispered.

Rhys sighed. "A hero, of course."

Rider grinned at me. "Our legends all have similar endings."

"The righteous versus the untenable," Rhys said.

I thought about the brothers and the story they'd told

about when they were boys—before the wolves had brought them to us. They'd been too young, Rhys had said. They'd not understood the superstitions of those around them, how the kingdom feared the power they shared. Their king had played upon that, and mere boys were suddenly to blame for all the misfortunes of their realm.

"There's something else," I said. "Your old staff, the one from your homelands." At Rhys' nod, I asked, "Could it be only coincidence that the frost monsters and winter sprites were so enamored with it?"

Rhys lifted a shoulder, an easy gesture that seemed more to fit someone like Steed than either of these two. "Coincidence seems unlikely, but they may have merely been drawn to the cold."

"Cold" was not how I would have described it. The brothers' magic felt different but not simply in its temperature. There was something else, something that lacked the bite and tingle of my magic—or, more precisely, the magic of those who had surrounded me.

My magic was something else entirely. I was of the light on my mother's side—her mother had been powerful, her magic radiant. And then there was Asher, one of the strongest beings in the realm, who was capable of harnessing the dark energy of his kind even before he'd gambled with spellcasting to garner more. I had an unusual heritage solely because my mother had been of both light and dark, able to access both. The fact that she'd carried me to term despite my human father was more than rare.

That had been Asher's doing. The previous Lord of the North had spent a century studying and learning from his failing attempts to cross bloodlines. There was a reason half-bloods were disdained. It wasn't natural. It never worked. The children of those couplings had died before being brought into this world, and so often, the mother had paid with her own life—except for Asher's children, several of whom had survived. And me, who'd surely had help from Asher and the elders when they'd brought my mother through childbirth, both of us alive.

Things had not gone so well with Ruby. Even though her mother had discovered the secret to bringing her to term, she'd miscalculated Ruby's uniqueness. It had not been only power Ruby had gained from the crossing. It had altered her very being, turned something fey into deadly venom. Ruby had poisoned her own mother.

I sighed, shaking off the thought. It didn't hurt the way it had before, but there was nothing to gain from living in the past. We would look forward. We would deal with what was at hand.

"So," I offered, "we continue to research base magic, the deadening of magic, and the possibility of the fey being able to use a connection to energy outside of that which resides beneath their lands."

Rider nodded. "And the humans."

I bit back a grimace. I had no interest in letting my guard study the humans, especially given the warnings of the elders and what they'd done at the boundaries. "It seems unsafe," I reminded him.

He inclined his head. "Old knowledge, then."

I raised my brow at the pile of scrolls on the table before him and smiled. "Seems like that will keep you busy for a while, in any case. I know you understand the importance of this. But if something were to happen to me and to Isa"—I swallowed hard, thinking of all the possibilities—"there would be nothing preventing the encroachment." Veil had been betrayed, trapped by his own willingness to bargain with me and to save his lands. But his heliotropes had turned on him, likely in no small part because of his favor toward me. But the fey were fools if they thought they could have done without him, because the bargain he'd made with me was the only thing capable of preventing their downfall and keeping the humans at bay.

There were only Isa and me to do that. "If we are gone, it will be the end of all fey."

4

THEA

THEA HAD MOSTLY KEPT HER PROMISE IN THE WEEKS FOLLOWING the night she'd embraced the knowledge that she'd made the right decision and accepted this corridor-filled castle as her home. Her superior had tested her more than once, but Thea was trying, and she found that she could tolerate a lot more of the man's ignorance than she'd believed possible.

Barris had helped. He and the other guards under the same lead didn't want the man's wrath any more than she, so Thea didn't feel bad about accepting the support when she did get stuck with extra tasks. She'd worked hard, she'd completed her duties, and she'd stayed away from the horses. Mostly.

More than anything else, she'd accepted that her life in the castle would not be that of her imaginings. It was something different but no less satisfying, and she would have to work her way up the chain like everyone else. Thea hoped she would someday be allowed to toil in the stable and maybe even eventually oversee the horses' care. But for the time being, she was content to train, to polish armor, and to mess each night with the members of her guard, which was why she stood slack-jawed when Edan called her to meet with one of the Seven.

"Thea," Edan repeated.

She shook herself, dropping the mace she'd been about to train with. It came perilously close to landing on the side of her foot. Barris laughed. She glanced at him sidelong, and he brushed his mouth with a gloved fist, wiping the smile from his face.

She looked back at Edan. "Yes, of course."

He nodded and turned without another word, and Thea stared at his back for a moment before Barris gestured her to follow. *Right*, she mouthed, still shocked.

The heat of the battle with the fey had worn off, and Thea's ambition to be a warrior had come to a stuttering halt once she'd had a few weapons lessons. She was out of her league. She wasn't ready. And as she followed Edan through a maze of corridors packed with castle staff going about their daily duties, she wondered briefly if it was another of those messes she tended to get herself into. As they traversed the first set of stairs, her stomach tightened, and her palms went slick at the second.

It was bad. It was one of their private corridors. It was the level that housed the high guard and the lord of the castle. Thea had never been there, but she'd known—everyone had. To enter those halls without approval could mean a swift death. *Of course*, she'd thought before, *because how else would they know who meant Freya harm?* But now, as her boots trod lightly over dark polished stone, Thea wasn't certain about anything.

Edan stopped at a carved stone doorway, tilting his head to shepherd her in.

She froze. Edan watched her. *Coward*, she thought, the hiss of anger moving her feet. She gave Edan a quick nod on her way through and strolled into a room the likes of which she'd never seen.

The castle floors below were grand and imposing, but the rooms were mostly utilitarian. She'd seen the banquet hall and the library—rooms meant to impress—but this was different. There were rich tapestries sewn to a skill that surpassed even Cora's. There were carved wood surfaces and ancient swords. Every inch of the space spoke of the ancients who'd ruled before and of legends. She wondered what she had expected. She was in the house of an elven lord.

"Thea," a voice snapped.

Thea's eyes were stolen from the grandeur by the impatient gestures of a familiar face. "Ruby," she said, breathing deeply.

"Yes," Ruby told her. "Of course." She flicked her fingers then slapped a hand on the long table she leaned against. "Come, see what I have for you."

Before the fey conflict, Thea hadn't seen Ruby in ages. She'd known her growing up, of course, but Ruby had not been one to find and keep friends. She'd kept to herself for long stretches of time and then would suddenly be there, the impetus of the party, weaving tales and pouring wine. Ruby had always had a wide-ranging network of traders and associates—she was no timid girl. But she chose who and when, and Thea had been more of a consistent acquaintance to Steed than to his sister. The current Ruby was not the Ruby she remembered.

Thea had known a wild-haired waif of a girl whose skin was covered in painted ivies, with pouches of tonics hanging over a tattered skirt. She'd worn bangles and eye tint and had twirled like her spirit could not be controlled. She'd been a feral, fire-throwing, untamable thing.

But Ruby had been tamed. Her bright curls were drawn

into tight braids, the slant of her ears on full display. She was slim in black leather with no adornments or jewels, no ribbons or lace. Her boots were flat, her fingers clean. She gestured to the parchment before her, a register written in her own hand. "This," she said. "Your list."

"My…" Thea stared down at Ruby. Ruby must have been confused, mistaken Thea for someone else. She did have a bit of a haggard look about her, something that spoke of lack of rest and too much work. Thea wondered if Ruby was well. She wondered if she was even allowed to ask her that. The strange new rules of Thea's position had tripped her up so many times that she could never be sure. She'd tightened her quick tongue, second-guessing every response.

Ruby nodded as if she'd not just lost her audience to the confusion. "Yes, your list." She straightened, touching a quill to her lips. She tapped it three times, apparently considering. "How good are you at climbing?"

"What?"

Ruby shook her head and scribbled something at the bottom of the list. "No matter. I'll find someone who is." She tossed the quill aside, rolling the parchment into a tidy scroll. "I'm afraid the windswheel is out of season, but seedlings will be fine. And I'm sure you know where to find the best yellowroot, and there's a stream that runs by Falcon Lake…"

"You want me to collect yellowroot?"

Ruby looked up, her expression harried.

"She wants to send you on a fool's errand," Steed said from behind them. "And I am that fool."

Thea turned, and Ruby said, "You'll go along with Steed. He's off to see Junnie and her new Council. While he's tending to business, you'll collect supplies and herbs from the gardens there so I can replenish my medicine stock. I've already sent word ahead of you." She tied a thin ribbon around the rolled document. "On your route, you can pick up the things from this list." She held the parchment up for Thea.

"But I—"

Ruby pushed the scroll into her hands. "You've been a healer for a long time, and you know the flora. Steed cannot do this for me, and we need it desperately. If I'd had it before —" She shook her head, but she'd not needed to say. Thea knew she was speaking of Grey. By all accounts, his wounds had healed, just not as well or as quickly as anyone would have liked. Fey fire could do that to a person. Ruby sent Steed a purposeful glare. "I'd do it myself, but they won't let me leave."

"You know why," he told her.

"Right," she chirped back, crossing her arms. "Which is why I've solved the problem for you." She smiled at Thea. "Do have fun, but remember I need these quickly."

Thea's fingers tightened around the rolled parchment, her gaze floating between Ruby and Steed. "Am I stepping into the middle of a family quarrel?"

Ruby hopped on to the massive table, crossing leg over knee. "It doesn't matter. You are of the guard now, so you do what they say."

Ruby smiled, but Thea could see there was truth behind it, though she didn't know how sending her along would solve Ruby's problem. Surely, the roots and leaves were not the intent.

"I will urge you one final time to reconsider," Steed told Ruby. His tone was amicable enough, but Ruby didn't budge.

"Off with you both," she answered, flipping her hands toward the door. "I have much to do."

Bewildered, Thea turned to go. Ruby called her name, and Thea glanced over her shoulder, seeing the two side by side. They no more appeared to be siblings than she and Cora.

Ruby's tone suddenly softened. "It was good to see you, Thea. Safe travels."

Thea nodded, her gaze falling on Steed.

"Go on ahead," he said, crossing his arms over his chest in the same stubborn manner his much-smaller sister. "I'll meet you in the stables as soon as I've finished up here."

5

FREY

RUBY'S OBSESSION WITH HEALING GREY AND, I SUSPECTED, A few ideas that might get her into trouble were heavily cutting into her time at my side. She'd managed to resolve her castle duties but not with the attention to detail she'd shown before. Grey had been healing, and though his wounds no longer caused him significant pain, we'd all been allowing Ruby leeway while she dealt with the aftermath of her guilt. Besides, the more she focused on Grey, the less chance she had to attempt to leave the castle on her own.

The remainder of my guard were healing well, thanks in no small part to the changeling Liana's help. Before she'd departed, she'd left supplies and instructions to aid each of them. No one had been foolish enough to believe it was out of the goodness of her heart, but she'd been well paid in trade, and we'd needed the help, even if she was only working to repair them for her own gain later. Anvil had been making the rounds in Camber with a small band of sentries, Rhys and Rider were researching ancient magics and possible solutions to our current problems, and my Second had been running the castle. That left me to answer to the clan leaders and conflicts, while only Steed was free to parley with Junnie so we might be able to keep tabs on the girl, Isa, and the humans in her care.

I tapped a finger against the carved arm of my throne. There had been whispers from the rogues that I should have let the humans come, let them destroy the base magic, and let the fey deal with their own troubles. And there had been word among a few in Camber that I'd handled the fey bargain poorly and that the way I'd dealt with Veil had been unbecoming for a lord.

I didn't appreciate the comparison, given how the previous lord had handled fey, but I was trying to take their opinions into consideration for how I would move forward. The rogues were wrong—the humans would not be merely a fey problem. Once their lands were dry of that power, the fey would do whatever it took to seek out more. The fact that we'd been in that situation at all should have been proof enough. And maybe I hadn't handled the bargain with Veil with enough tact, but he'd tricked us into being under his thumb. He'd known the others would come for Ruby and that I would have to answer their attack. He'd let it play out to benefit himself and his kingdom.

I stared out at the waiting faces of my audience. Whatever Veil thought of the bargain we'd made, what was done was done. I had no cause to go back on my word, and as long as Isa could handle the humans, I would be able to stay at my post, protecting and ruling the North.

As such, I'd been unable to travel to the outer lands to see her progress. My guard was scattered and healing, the fey had not yet settled, and the only way through was with the guarantee of safe passage by the high fey lord himself, something I had no interest in attempting any time soon.

Junnie had left soldiers and sent occasional watchmen and would soon be journeying there herself. Isa had not been alone in her new task. But I trusted only Junnie outside of my own guard, and she'd had more than her share of work building a new Council to govern her lands and keep her own people in check. Isa being away had eased some of the dissent Junnie was facing among her new Council. They'd not wanted the girl to die because of their reverence for her connection with beasts, but they'd certainly not wanted a creature who was half human and half dark elf at their Council head's right hand.

Steed had been trading throughout the lands since he was young, and he could get along with—or at least bargain with—nearly anyone. But there was another reason he'd been my choice to meet with Junnie. Easygoing as he seemed, he had a surprising intuition about those who were not. He'd realized things about Junnie and had spoken his concern more than once. He'd had things to say about her gift, which seemed to favor canines in the way mine favored birds, and things about Isa, namely that she did not appear to have an affinity for either. I would not have called him a spy by any means, but it was nice to have someone along who noticed people's tells and recognized their motives, especially when I was bound to the obligations of my throne.

"Dagan of Camber," Kieran announced, calling forward the next name on his list. I inclined my head toward Dagan in acknowledgment of his station and my respect for it. The throne room was enormous, with high arched ceilings and a long open space, and Kieran's voice echoed despite the walls being wreathed in burgundy and velvet. Intricate stone constructs bore torches, their flickering light throwing moving shadows throughout the room.

I sat near the back wall, my throne on a raised platform overlooking it all.

Dagan did not bow. He simply stated his grievance and how he expected it to be resolved.

"Done," I said, gesturing for Kieran to see that it was. Dagan was no fool—he knew what to expect under our laws and had only asked for as much. But he didn't favor me, and I had no interest in furthering that discontent with someone who held clout within Camber. "Anvil reports that the rebuilding is going well," I offered. "Please let us know if there is any way the people of Camber can be additionally assisted."

"Aye," Dagan said, inclining his head. "All is well. It is not the worst we have seen."

"Nonetheless," I said, biting back whatever else I might have said at the reminder of the massacre from long ago.

Dagan turned to go, and at my left, Kieran called the next clan leader—a rogue, from the looks of it. My day consisted of constant managing of life and order.

Ruby slipped into place beside me. "It comes with the uniform," she said. "The guard has never claimed one who was merely a fighter. If you want to choose the dead, you have to manage the living. It keeps us from turning murderous."

I smiled at her words, the sentiment one I'd shared with her after I'd been restored to the throne and she was learning what it meant to be one of my Seven. "Mostly not murderous," I amended.

She stared across the throne room, and I knew she'd not taken it as jest. Ruby had intentions that would not end well for at least one of the parties involved.

My guard looked less and less fey each day she stood as part of my rule. Her face was still angled and her ears sharp, but Ruby was not one of them. It didn't stop her from thinking of it, though, or from researching. Ruby was constantly trying to understand the fey, but they didn't think linearly. It was impossible to know what each desired until they found a pinnacle and became obsessed to the point that their obsession showed. Then there were those who excelled at deceit and trickery. It was not something she could learn or control.

But I glanced at her speculatively, because Ruby had foreseen much more than any of us had known. She'd laid into place what she thought she needed to defeat plans the rest of us were entirely unaware of, and I was grateful for it.

"I hope you do not intend to act on whatever is boiling beneath your surface," I told her.

She met my eyes evenly. "I would never endanger my home."

It was not precisely a denial, but at least she was firm in her allegiance—that the castle and its people were her home in a way Ruby had never truly had before. I glanced at Kieran, and he called the next in line.

When we'd finally exhausted the list, I turned to Ruby again. "Are you up for working out some aggression?" She eyed me questioningly, and I explained, "Chevelle would like us to meet him in the training room to check on a few new recruits."

Her brow quirked at the possibility, and then Ruby straightened her whip to lead us from the room.

6

THEA

THEA STOOD JUST INSIDE THE STABLE ENTRANCE, A NEATLY rolled cloak in hand. She'd tucked the scroll into a hidden inside pocket along with a charcoal nub for marking off the items Ruby had requested as they were collected. She'd worn her guard-issued clothes and two short knives, and a pair of canteens was strapped over her shoulder. She felt bare holding nothing aside from that cloak, and she wondered what else she was forgetting to bring. She made her way to the tack room, a neatly arranged collection of riding gear in leather and metal that would be no help at all. Walking farther down the aisle, she glanced into the feed stores, deciding that the woven sacks might be helpful in her collection. Steed would have thought of that, surely. *But what if we found something that needed separating from the other supplies?* Ruby's list had certainly contained items that should not be stored in close contact with one another—or with anyone's person, really.

Thea folded the sacks and tucked them into her cloak. At the end of the aisle, she found an empty bench inside one of the shadowed stalls. She sat, making herself comfortable while she waited for Steed to arrive.

It took longer than she expected.

THEA WOKE, not realizing that she'd fallen asleep. In the quiet warmth, she'd drifted off, the roll of her cloak behind her head. Something had shifted in the darkness and caused her to jolt awake, a tingling sensation in her arms and hands her only clue she'd drifted into slumber. She wiped a thin line of drool off her cheek.

"Sorry," she said with a cough, sitting upright to blink at Steed. "I just—I was just waiting on you here."

He leaned forward from the shadows to take her erstwhile pillow, and Thea saw the twitch of his lip. "You've got hay in your hair."

She stood, brushing a hand over the mess of her braids. It was matted and pulling loose, with frayed strands here and there. Thea looked over her shoulder, but there was no hay in sight. Someone must have tucked it there while she slept. *Barris*, she thought, but only briefly because her captain was already halfway down the aisle. She ran after him.

Five horses stood at the entrance to the stables, and ten more with mounted soldiers were in the courtyard. Thea's gaze caught a familiar movement, a recognizable shift of posture she'd seen before. Barris. She glared at him. He smiled.

Steed was tying Thea's parcel onto her horse, and she took a moment to straighten the worst of her braid. "They are all going with us."

He didn't turn around. "The high guard will not travel alone, for the time being."

More rules, Thea thought. She wondered if it had always been like this, with Ruby under lock and key and Steed unable to leave on his own. She was nearly positive that the answer was no. She remembered visits from the Seven when she'd lived in Camber. They often traveled in pairs, but they did occasionally arrive on their own. "Because of the fey?" she whispered.

Steed turned, his situating of her saddle and parcel complete. "Thea, we aren't going to have problems, are we?"

She knew what he meant: her cursed mouth. She opened it to reply but snapped it shut again, deciding to heed Barris's relentless advice: *just do your duty and keep it sealed.*

Thea wondered if she was meant to be with the others, but as she mounted, she saw their armor and swords. They were soldiers, she realized. She was a meager assistant among the guard. They were there to protect the high guard, and if anything were to happen, they would probably have to protect her as well. She cursed herself for only bringing the short knives. She might have been terrible with a sword, but she could at least have brought her bow.

The armed soldiers split, and two rode ahead while the others waited to bring up the rear of the party. A tall sentry mounted one of the five horses Steed had readied, and Thea recognized him as Duer. She'd crossed paths with the man before—he'd trained the new recruits with axes and hammers, and Thea had kept her distance to work instead with knives. She'd seen what a hammer could do to a person. Both weapons were capable of making a kill, but a knife blade was sharp, the cut clean. A slash could be stitched back together, but a blow by a hammer was a mess of a thing.

They rode out with two of the horses empty of burden. Thea understood those were backup in case anything went wrong.

It didn't help to rally her courage. She was quiet as they rode through the castle gates, past the staff and visitors who nodded their respect. Dressed in the uniform of a guard, with Steed more her superior and less her childhood friend, Thea felt the weight of it all. Even if she'd committed herself to her new life, she still felt strange, being a member of the castle guard, though that out-of-the-ordinary sensation wasn't unpleasant.

The horses picked up speed, and she drew in a deep breath of the cool mountain air, smiling like a fool. After galloping through some rough mountain passes, Thea realized that the men she was with had not been picked for their sword-fighting abilities. They were horsemen, soldiers who could ride. They must have been chosen personally by Steed. The procession made faster time than she'd imagined possible, slowing only to cross the occasional stream. They might have taken the long route, bringing them past the water onto easily passable ground, but she was glad they didn't.

The beast beneath her leapt over trees, cracking low limbs and startling fauna without so much as a flinch. He jumped with abandon into the occasional creek, spraying water, flinging mud, and snorting at will. It was exhilarating after weeks spent in the castle, scraping and cleaning and trudging up the stairs. Thea missed the outdoors, even if she'd spent much time in the open sky. She'd missed the wind, the air, and the thin mountain trees.

It wasn't her alone, either. She saw in the others a freeing of their posture, an ease of their smiles.

Especially in Steed—his rigid bearing was gone, and he seemed so much more the boy he used to be. Thea wasn't certain it was simply the air, though, because Steed had been born to handle the creatures who carried them down the mountain pass. He had never been more at home than he was with his stock. She had wondered if he'd missed it, but Thea could see how his new life meant more. He had a bit of both worlds just then, and his animals were important for more than merely companionship and trading.

When they'd been children, Thea had not understood Steed's connection with the beasts. She loved horses, unquestionably, but she loved all animals. Steed's relationship with them was different. It was in his blood. His ancestors had traded and bred, bringing together new lines that surpassed all the old. It was a thing of beauty to watch him train a horse. It was beyond beautiful to really see the bond he held with his own.

They rode past nightfall then took camp near a copse of narrow trees. The soldiers quickly dismounted, drawing their gear from the horses and going to task. Thea slid more slowly from her own mount, surreptitiously stretching her legs. She couldn't recall when she'd last ridden so tirelessly and remembered that it had been when they'd raced to meet the rest of the Seven on fey lands. The excitement of that ride had numbed her. Fear of imminent death apparently had a way of overshadowing the need to stretch.

She heaved her gear from the horse's back, bringing it to rest beside one of the trees. Steed settled his there as well, obviously not as weary as she. She'd forgotten she meant not to speak freely and asked, "Why do you still ready the horses yourself? Don't you have plenty of hands for that?"

Steed brushed a clump of mud from his trousers. "We aren't at home now, and this isn't like Camber. Take care to mind things yourself, and you'll know they're done correctly."

She laughed, wondering when he'd become that much of a perfectionist. But he only watched her, his expression grave, and she understood. "You mean it's the only way you'll know you're safe." She'd gone pale—she knew she had—but there was nothing to be done for it.

"You joined the guard, Thea. Surely, you understood there'd be risk."

She swallowed. "I did. Of course. I just—I mean, I thought you'd be safe among your own men."

"I trust them with my life," he told her. "That doesn't mean I wouldn't take that gamble into my own hands whenever I'm given the chance."

"Right," she said. "Of course." She was repeating herself, which wasn't a good sign. She sighed. "So, this list..."

"Yes," Steed answered, gesturing high into the air above. Thea's gaze followed, finding only a clouded sky and the tips of those narrow trees. "That," he told her, "is where we'll need to ascend."

Her automatic response caught in her throat as she remembered Ruby's words: *Can you climb?* She stared at Steed, wide-eyed.

He smirked. "That's what you get for joining in league with my sister."

Thea stuttered, but Steed only turned and headed toward the ring, where the others were building a fire. "See you at daybreak," he called over his shoulder.

Thea's gaze rose again to the skyline, to the tips of those trees, and she swallowed the nasty lump in her throat. She'd done it again, leapt head-first into a tangle of briars.

THE NEXT MORNING, well before the rising sun, Thea and the others had cleared their camp. The horses were saddled, breakfast was had, and a young, thin sentry was scaling his way up the tall thornberry tree by rope and foot. It seemed well and good, but Thea knew that at some point, he would reach the buds Ruby needed and would have to let the rope free to gain use of his hands. They were not to be tainted by spells or magic, Ruby had said. It was to be done by hand.

It was not something Thea especially wanted to see.

She had not intended to show doubt but couldn't quite muster the strength to stand beneath that tree. She ran a hand over her horse as the others waited below, shouting cheers and taunts to a sentry they seemed to know well. The sentry called out when he'd secured his prize then slowly made his way down the tree. There were words of approval and pats on the back all around before the men returned to their mounts.

Steed handed Thea the small pouch to inspect their spoils. She split a pod open with her thumb then glanced up at Steed. "Perfect. Ruby will be pleased."

He smirked. "I wouldn't expect too much from her until Grey is mended, but this should help."

"She blames herself," Thea said.

Steed's brow drew down.

She kept forgetting to keep her trap shut. "Sorry," she told him. "It's none of my business." She drew the list from her pocket, scratching off one item out of eight and twenty.

"She does," Steed said. "Some people always take the guilt onto themselves." Thea looked up at him, and he added, "And then there are those who simply draw trouble."

She was pretty sure she'd taken offense to that, but she didn't have a chance to get the declaration out. She glared at Steed's back as he rode away on his horse.

Barris rode past her, leaning down to say, "I've some free advice for the taking—"

She cut him off. "I know. Keep it sealed."

He chuckled, and Thea climbed onto her own horse. They rode again through the day, swiftly and surely, not stopping until well after dark. Thea could smell the lake in the cool air, though clouds obscured the light of the moon. She'd traveled the mountain before and had been to the base of it and farther into the grasslands and forests nearing Council lands. Her work as a healer had brought her there, but Thea hadn't minded the journey. It had been stirring to see the land and to be out of Camber for a few days at a time.

It was different, though, as a member of the castle guard. It made her more vulnerable, because there was an importance to her station she'd never had. But it also made her safer, because sentries and soldiers rode at her side. Of all the places Thea had been or had ever imagined going, she never had the idea she would one day walk into the heart of Council lands. And she could not have fathomed it would be dressed as a castle guard.

"Finally quiet," Barris said from beside her.

She elbowed him in the ribs.

He smiled, drawing her saddle free to put with the others. "Come, eat with us. We've found a nice spot by the bank."

She eyed him suspiciously. "Who's getting pushed in?"

Barris shook his head. "Not when we're on a mission. Some of us prefer not to get reprimands."

Thea crossed her arms and leaned toward him. "Some of you just get lucky you don't get caught."

Barris winked. "You call it luck. I call it expertise." Barris suddenly straightened, and Thea turned to see Steed in the shadows, watching them as he tended one of the horse's legs. Barris nodded respectfully and gestured Thea toward the lake.

"You go on," she told him. "I want to see if I can be of help."

When he left, Thea made her way through the tall grass, careful not to startle the horse, even if she'd yet to see one twitch at a sudden movement. She might have asked if she could be of assistance but instead only watched Steed as he slid a palm over the animal's leg, making occasional soothing noises. She knelt at a distance, waiting.

Steed shifted, and his touch became a gentle stroke. "Nothing serious. Just a tangle with a snapped branch. He'll be fine."

That was good. They were too far out to do much for the animal if he had been badly injured.

Thea moved closer, letting the gelding sniff at her hair. She rubbed curled fingers against its jaw, and it blew into her hair. She smiled—she couldn't help it.

Steed was watching her, both of them kneeling in the high grass. "What?" she asked him.

He shook his head, as if maybe he hadn't realized he'd been doing it. "I haven't seen you in so long. Before all this, I mean. How many seasons has it been?"

She pursed her lips. "Maybe three seasons before the one when we heard you'd joined the guard." She looked at him. "Everyone was quite surprised at that."

He laughed, the sound short and quiet. "No more surprised than I, I would imagine."

Thea ran a hand over the horse's snout, up and under his mane. The gelding leaned into it. "And yet less surprised than Ruby?"

Steed's gaze narrowed on her.

She shrugged. "The entire town was saying it. You know her reputation."

He did. She could see that much was true. But he didn't confirm or deny his sister's involvement. Even if Ruby had planned it, he'd had the choice. He could have walked away, refused to help.

Thea thought of Freya and then of the young girl Isa and her wide, dark eyes. *No,* she supposed, *he probably couldn't have refused.* "There's something very... enthralling about all of this, is there not?"

He smiled at her. "Yes. I've found I'm quite unable to return to my previous life."

"Me too," she agreed. "Quite."

"And do you fancy yourself a warrior someday?"

He was teasing her—she was sure of it. But Thea didn't mind. Steed's banter had never held ill intent. "If I could hold a sword, I'd be your girl."

She'd said it playfully enough, but there was something in the phrase that was not entirely right. Not there, alone in the low light, away from the others. She might have wished she hadn't, but the look on Steed's face sent a tingling heat through her—a response she should absolutely not be directing toward a superior.

Thea stood, brushing a hand across her leg. "Are you coming for dinner?"

"Go ahead," he told her. "I'll be along in a bit."

She turned, avoiding the chance to speak again. She couldn't seem to trust her foolish mouth.

7

FREY

CHEVELLE AND I STOOD BENEATH THE LEDGE OF THE HIGH windows of the training room where we'd spent so many days of our youth. Those unruly children were gone, replaced by the Lord of the North and her Second. We shared a glance, and he surreptitiously slid his collar between forefinger and thumb.

I smiled at the signal, a secret just between us from so long ago. I gestured toward Ruby, who stood not far from me with her new charge. "Are you certain we need more fire around here?"

Chevelle chuckled, but both of us knew the duty would serve a higher purpose. Ruby could train the new sentries who excelled in flamework without the risk of being burned, certainly, but in doing so, we'd given her one more task to keep her occupied with something other than vengeance.

Ruby's new charge was petite, not much taller than Ruby herself, and built of nothing but lean muscle. Her arms were bare beneath a black-leather vest, aside from short bracers at her wrists. Her cropped hair was spiky and glossy black, and her dark eyes tipped up at the edges as if in a smile. But she was not smiling. She was a warrior.

Ruby snapped her fingers again, bringing the girl's focus to her at once. "There is no place for showmanship in a true fight. It matters not how impressive your flame looks when you're defending your home." The girl stared at Ruby, attentiveness her only response. "Make it hot and make it clean. As fast as you can with a single focus, a steady point." Ruby gestured in the air between them, a jab with her hand like that of a blade.

The girl drew one foot back to ready her stance, waiting for the command to go.

"She's good," I murmured to Chevelle at my side.

He nodded once. "Willa, she's called. From a clan south of Camber."

"And what of the others?"

"Edan has recommended three, and there are two more I've an eye on myself."

It was no surprise—the head of the guard didn't recommend anyone for higher service unless he was absolutely certain of their abilities. He wasn't willing to stake his reputation on mere potential. Chevelle tended toward a surety of character sooner, though his ruling was more often a bit sharp.

"What about Barris?" I asked.

Chevelle kept his gaze on Ruby and her charge. "He's doing well. Solid strength and an even temperament."

"He doesn't carry his mother's talent?"

"Not that I've seen."

I nodded, remembering the wall of wind that had saved us so long ago. She'd given her life for it, but the strength Barris's mother had wielded was extraordinary. "And the healer?"

He pressed his lips together, glanced at me sidelong. "Thea. Ruby has sent her along with Steed."

I blinked slowly and resisted the urge to press my fingers to the bridge of my nose or to say anything with her in earshot.

Chevelle let the corner of his mouth tip up at my response. "She's gathering supplies for Ruby. As a healer, she has knowledge that many of the others do not."

I nodded. "It's just as well," I said. "I don't mind the idea of a healer being along with the group."

"If I'm not mistaken," he said, "he's chosen Barris to go along as well."

"I wonder how she finds the time to be so clever," I mused, watching the smallest and possibly most dangerous of my Seven.

Chevelle's expression said he did not think *clever* was the proper word.

Ruby and the girl continued their honing of her talent, and when Kieran appeared in one of the arched doorways, Chevelle and I met him halfway across the open floor.

"An urgent matter calls at the gate." His expression grim, Kieran explained, "A few rogues barreled over a clan east of the mountain, killing stock and wounding men, and the victims are demanding retribution and an immediate audience with the Lord of the North."

Chevelle waited in stillness, showing no apparent intention of allowing me to be called to the gate. "None are entitled to demand anything of an elven lord," he started, but I held up a hand to stop him.

"We've time," I said. "Let us go see what the rogues have stirred up now."

8

THEA

THE NEXT FEW DAYS CARRIED ON WITH LONG RIDES, LATE nights, and Thea collecting items from Ruby's list. When they finally neared the village that housed the new Council, the bags of plants, seeds, and supplies were stuffed to full and smelled strongly of sap and decomposition. Thea suspected she might be beginning to as well. She would wait for a bath and a change of clothes, though, because the woodlands were thick there, the trees too close. Even in the clearings, those wide grass fields dotted with bright summer blooms, Thea felt overwhelmed by the greenery, the growth, the suffocating proximity of it all.

She and the others had been raised on the mountain, with stone and packed earth beneath their feet. The trees had been tall and thin, narrow enough to embrace and to see past and know what was coming. The trunks of the trees near the village, even the wild growth not aided by the hands of elves, were massive things, dark and misshapen. It felt as if creatures and beasts surrounded them, towering high and twisting to

51

block out the sun like the dragons of old fey lore. Thea didn't like it one bit.

The sun shone brightly in those fields, though, the open space becoming frequent enough that Thea had to pull at the material of her shirt just to get enough air and relief from the warmth. Eventually, the trees became less threatening but no less bizarre. Squat trunks as wide as ten horses had been carved into homes with smooth, bark-edged windows and arched doors, moss-covered stones, and ivy entangled into the designs. Thea had always heard the light elves did not approve of the lavish constructions of the North, but she did not believe these were any less excessive. They might be able to claim their structures were not as flashy, but it ended there. They were plainly meant to impress, the details so extreme and unnecessary on one in particular that she nearly hadn't noticed the man peering from beneath its moss-coated shutters, glaring at them.

Unnerved, Thea glanced at Steed. He rode on, his gaze ahead, but he held that rigid posture again, the High Guard bearing that they all seemed to have, as though he was aware of the slight but above it. Duer apparently had no such compunction—he stared directly back at the man. Thea smiled, satisfied with both Duer's and Steed's responses, and watched as the dwelling's shutters snapped closed.

There were more structures along the way, some deep within the earth and camouflaged beneath fern and briar, and some high in tree boughs, with ladders and bridges grown between their doors. Others were built within massive root systems, tall enough to stable horses and wide enough for their entire group. The majority were ordinary trees, though, adorned with only hangings and quilts, flowering plants vining prettily up their bases to taper into nothing at about mid-waist. Thea saw that the showy structures in the forests surrounding the village were outliers. The village itself was a bright, open pathway with homes that were not much more than what was needed for shelter, and the overgrowth hadn't taken over the community's layout.

It was not until they were at the village center and she'd seen the buildings of the Council that Thea understood what true grandeur the light elves were capable of. Anyone who'd been in range of the buildings would never have given stock to the idea that light elves were humble. Marbled columns and carved archways rose over a low-walled structure, ivies woven into a delicate canopy shading it all. Narrow windows looked out into the village, and movement inside indicated that the building was not short but buried half beneath the earth. Thea remembered, then, the stories she'd heard the season Freya had reclaimed her throne.

The Council villages had all been burned, razed to the ground by the other in Freya and Junnie's line. Francine, the child whom lord Asher had thought ungifted, shunned for her dull features and apparent lack of magic, had gone into a rage and destroyed the homes of High Council, Grand Council, and nearly everyone in between. Those who were in power had taken flight, gathering at a temple farther north. It had not saved them, though, for that was where they'd met with Lord Freya and the others and where the fighters of the North finally took their stand. The North had crushed them. Freya, a small, half-human girl so rich with power it had nearly broken her, had taken command.

Thea glanced at Barris where he rode with the others, sitting tall and proudly in the new uniform of that same elven lord. It seemed an unfriendly gesture, she thought, to send the boy whose parents had fought those councilmen, whose parents had *died* in that battle, along with them. It might not have been the same Council, but its subjects had buried their families, loved ones who had died at the hands of the men Thea rode with into their village, unescorted, to meet with their new Council head.

It had not been Junnie's decision which men would accompany their party, but Thea doubted she would approve of the message it sent. Or maybe she would, because it was a reminder of why they needed to partner with the new Northern lord and of what Junnie's allies could do. Thea felt ill. She was fairly certain it was the politics of it all and not the hasty breakfast she'd gulped down while collecting ratweed.

Steed drew his horse to a stop before the new Council building's grand entrance, and Thea and Duer came up on either side. She felt suddenly out of place there, despite having traveled at Steed's side when they'd last come to find Junnie before riding brazenly into fey lands.

Something had shifted during Thea's time at the castle, and she understood the training and organization of the guard. She didn't flinch, though, because regardless of her rank, Thea had been sent as emissary by one of the Seven, and there was no higher order among her company aside from the Lord herself.

"Steed," Junnie said, appearing not from within the doors of the Council building but from somewhere beside them, a half-dozen assistants in tow. She gestured for him to dismount, and first Steed then Duer did so. Thea followed suit, though the remainder of the guard waited on horseback. One of Junnie's men led their horses away to be brushed and watered, and Thea stood alone as Steed and Duer moved forward to meet with Junnie.

"Come," Junnie told them, moving with a grace and ease that suggested either comfort—a surety in her safety—or the desperation caused by knowing she had to appear as such. She wore long, decorative robes, each inlaid with the finest stitching. Her hair was startlingly blond, pulled back into loose braids with a little wisp that had come free to curl beside her bright-blue eyes.

These people all had the look of polished jewels, dazzling, vivid, and sharp. Thea had heard the sort of words the light elves used when speaking of her own kind: dark, dirty, and cold, and the words didn't refer to the stone of their mountain home. The light elves disdained everything about the dark, as if they were purer, their magic cleaner. They seemed to assume that their rules and codes occupied a moral high ground.

Thea knew about honor and principles. It was clear to her which side was truly corrupt.

"Thea," Junnie called to her. For an instant, Thea worried that her thoughts had shown on her face, but Junnie's expression was, by all outward appearances, warm, genuine, and kind. Junnie gestured toward a thin girl at her side. "This is Aster. She will assist you in your task."

The girl stepped forward, bobbing in a sort of curtsey, and Thea inclined her head in response.

"I've had them cull what could be readied beforehand, but Ruby was quite adamant in her missive that several items were to be cut and kept as fresh as possible. Please do let me know if there's anything else you might need."

"Thank you," Thea told her. "I'm certain it's greatly appreciated."

Junnie smiled. "So I've been assured." She led Steed and Duer away, and Thea stared blankly at them as they departed, still not entering the grand building before them.

"Dame Thea," the girl said.

"Thea will do." The girl's bright eyes fell, and Thea added, "If you please."

She glanced over her shoulder, finding Barris and the

others still ahorse, lined up in a simple formation, clearly suffering in the terrible heat. She looked back to Aster, wondering if the girl had just taken her first big charge as well. "Shall we?"

The girl's hands were long and graceful, gesturing ahead of them as she led the way. "Our gardens have been prepared by the most capable hands in the realm, tended to night and day to develop only the best of each variety. The main gardens house over a hundred species alone, and three other grounds have been set aside for specialties…"

No, Thea thought as the girl continued, *not her first big charge.* She eyed the girl's straight shoulders and easy pace. Thea didn't think she even rated as interesting in Aster's book.

They passed through several ivory columns draped with delicate flowering vines, the posts signifying the entry to the gardens, according to her host. Aster led them farther, her thin-soled shoes padding lightly over a natural path. The greenery became thicker as the foliage built up higher and higher before falling again to reveal a set of towering ivory walls. The garden, Aster explained, was as protected as any of the precious documents and scrolls.

"But they are seeds," Thea said. "As renewable in your hands as any—"

The girl's cold look cut her short. It was wrong, that expression on such a sweet little face, but Thea could see the ice there was true. "Dark magic," Aster said, "can make even the strongest seed no more than ash."

Fire. She'd meant Francine's fire, the burning of the villages. Questions flared in Thea's mind, but she bit her tongue. It was clearly a sore subject for the girl, and there was no doubt where she placed the blame.

Thea followed silently as Aster took them through an exquisite gateway. "This is our new garden," Aster said, pride warring in her tone with what might have been loss. Or Thea might have been imagining things again.

"It is the loveliest I have ever seen," Thea told her, and she meant it, not simply because she'd never seen a Council garden but because the entire space before them was designed as a labyrinth of beautiful flora. Woven lattices stretched skyward, balanced with blooms. Carved archways loomed overhead, dripping with green moss that shaded ferns and delicate blossoms below. As they moved through the twisting pathways, pools came into view, seemingly watched over by shaped brush in the forms of everything from dragons to butterflies.

Thea had never seen so much variety in her life, let alone in a single day. She stared, awestruck by variations she'd not known possible—red honeysuckle, freesia buds as big as her fist, leaves with white-tipped spikes, and thorns that dripped a black-violet slime. Her fingers drew in reflexively as she remembered the warnings she'd heard when she was younger. The light elves did not just possess the capacity for beauty. They created poisons as well.

She glanced up from the splendor and found Aster watching her with a thin smile. Thea had a momentary image of Isa, the young halfling girl who was strong and wild enough to keep the humans at bay, and made a vow to remember something else: *Don't underestimate anyone.*

RUBY

RUBY'S TIME WITH WILLA HAD PROVEN FRUITFUL. THE GIRL HAD been able to focus her power to a precise point right away, and with only the slightest guidance from Ruby, she began to understand the ways in which it could be manipulated further, twisted around and through the root of her energy for a more solid strike. Ruby could tell she would not be simply deadly but unswerving in both endurance and calm.

"Now, then," Ruby offered, "shall we break for mess?"

Willa stepped from her ready stance into a straighter posture and inclined her head.

It seemed she was a girl of few words. Ruby liked that too. She grinned at Willa, indicating for her to follow as Ruby spun toward the door. "Something special tonight, I think," she said to no one, her pace steady on the cold stone floor. After a brief stop at the kitchen to get a satchel of meat and breads, Ruby tossed Willa one bright-red apple and bit the other between her teeth. She winked at the girl, gesturing again as they made their way through the corridors. *Silent*, as she'd requested, and the girl's slim boots were no louder than a light summer breeze.

Ruby wrapped the satchel over an arm and shoulder, glancing back to be certain no one else was near. She bit harder into what was left of the apple, lifting her booted foot high onto the windowsill. She didn't have to question whether the girl would follow—she could tell by the look in her eyes. There was no fear, only eagerness and a thirst for more.

Ruby crawled hand over fist past the carved stone of the castle tower. She could feel Willa behind her, keeping pace without a sound. Ruby reached from stone to stone and drew herself over the final ledge. She turned to find the shorn-haired girl determinedly climbing onto the same small ledge.

Ruby let her do it herself. The wind was biting so high up but not unbearable, as it had been in previous seasons. She unlaced the strap of the satchel from around her arm and drew the bag open to grab two pieces of bread. Ruby set her apple on the ledge between them as she settled to sit with her legs over the ledge. She stared out into the western sky.

Willa followed suit, setting her apple core beside Ruby's, the bite impressions noticeably dissimilar. Ruby tapped her own apple, looking at the girl to be sure she was understood. "Never eat after me. Never touch the tips of my arrows or blades."

The girl looked back, and though Ruby could be certain the request was understood, she could not tell whether Willa had truly known, had heard the stories.

They each took a bite of their bread and looked toward the sky, clouded as it was with patches of fog.

They sat for nearly an hour, eating their fill in companionable silence.

Then Ruby heard the whispered warning—the purr and swish of a pixie—and she knew she'd made a mistake.

10

THEA

THEA HAD COLLECTED SEEDLINGS AND CUTTINGS WITH ASTER for the remainder of the day and neatly packed and sorted each one before Aster showed her to her quarters. The building was on the outskirts of the village and appeared to be set up similarly to their castle barracks. Aster had explained that it was where she and the rest of the guard would stay, but Thea understood she'd meant they were expected to remain there. They weren't under lock and key, but they were evidently unwelcome elsewhere.

"Thank you," she'd told the girl, not for the first time, then Aster had curtsied and walked away.

Thea stood outside the squat building made of earth and stone, staring not toward the village but at the darkening woods beyond. The village fires were far behind her, their flickering light barely illuminating the leaves and trees. The narrow spaces between those massive trunks were dark as pitch, depthless doorways into a thick forest devoid of sky. Thea had never felt so far from home.

Something moved within the shadows, and the glint of fire

caught on metal, momentarily lighting a thin strip of steel orange before it was gone.

Thea's hand slid to her belt, and she wrapped her fingers tightly around the handle of one of her short blades. She should have felt safe and protected there, but she was moving toward the trees, her feet light as she stepped over the rocks and moss at the base of their houses.

There were tangled briars between the back of their building and the tree line, so she went wide, her pace quick until she was behind the cover of a large oak tree. The scent of the forest was heavy as she held her knife close, remaining still to listen. Sounds echoed through the trees but only those of natural fauna. *Maybe not natural,* Thea thought, because there seemed to be an unnatural quantity of the little creatures, squirrels and birds and everything small without fear of attack. It was if they knew they were safe from the light elves who lived there, knew that no beast would be unnecessarily harmed.

She stared into the darkness, searching, then leaned forward to see around the tree. A hand slipped suddenly over her mouth, and before she could so much as gasp, it was covered, and a second hand closed over her empty fist and pulled it tightly against her chest.

She'd been disarmed, captured as quickly as a breath. She jerked, thrusting her other elbow backward, and was rewarded by being pressed harder against the tree. Thea raised her foot as high as she could and went to push off the tree.

"Hush," a voice whispered against her ear. "You'll rouse the guard."

Steed. It was Steed. With her heart thundering, Thea relaxed into his grip, sucking a much-needed lungful of air in through her nose. Steed released his hold on her mouth but stayed pressed behind her. "What are you doing?" he hissed.

"I just"—Thea swallowed—"I was following a strange figure into a darkened wood."

He moved back from her. "With no more than a short knife at your hip."

She started to argue that, in fact, she had *two* short knives, but she thought better of it. She caught her breath, leaning against the tree as Steed bent down to pick up her discarded knife. Even in the darkness, she could see the narrow-eyed look he gave her.

"I know," she told him. "I'm not in Camber anymore. I'm a member of the guard."

"Curiosity does not fare well—"

"I wasn't curious," she whispered, not meaning to interrupt him but apparently unable to stop herself. "I had a bad feeling is all."

Steed leaned close to her, his voice still low. "Then you signal your guard."

She crossed her arms. "You're out here alone."

"I can use a sword." He gestured toward the darkness. "And I'm not alone."

Thea felt the blood rush to her cheeks. Someone had seen her mistake, someone other than Steed, who didn't tend to tell everyone when he saw a person act the fool.

Steed nodded. "Duer and I are handling Council business. So if you'd like to return to your quarters…"

Thea felt sick. "Of course. I'm sorry." She turned, rushing toward the distant lights.

"Thea," Steed said to her back. She glanced over her shoulder, catching the flash of his dark eyes. "Sword practice. Tonight."

She started to respond to say, "Yes, of course," but he was

gone, disappeared into the dark of the forest. She stared after him, listening for some sign of him or the other man. All she heard were the night creatures, scratching and flapping and chirping as if no danger was in sight.

~

THEA RETURNED to find that her guard had built a fire outside of their quarters and were gathering around it, engaged in various trivial tasks. Apparently, she'd not been the only one discontented or ill at ease. Barris looked up at her from across the firelight, giving her a smile and a tilt of his head. *Where have you been?* the look said.

She would be damned if she would tell him. She wasn't about to admit that to anyone. "Barris," she said in greeting, skipping any chance he might have of pressing her for information. "Care to teach me a little about swords?"

His eyes laughed at her, but the rest of him managed to hold it in. "I believe we can handle that," he answered. "Any particular area you're interested in?"

She straightened as he stood to face her, his own sword ready at his hip. "All of it."

"Aye," he told her. "I suppose it is about time, now that they've got you running with this lot."

Thea suspected Barris didn't mean himself and the other guards. He meant the Seven, running errands for Ruby, and riding at the head of the group with Steed. She would be a target, or she would be a casualty by proximity. Or worse: a liability.

They worked long into the night, crossing swords and perfecting her grip. She was terrible, and she knew it, but Barris assured her that with a proper sword—one built for her tall, lean frame—she'd be able to wield one well enough.

Thea understood that "well enough" was not what would keep her alive. "Well enough" would only delay the inevitable, and if no other sentries were near if she was attacked, she would be finished. Her family had been right—she was a healer, not a fighter. But being wrong had never stopped her before.

"Again," she told Barris, returning to her starting stance.

He frowned at her attempt. "Maybe we've been going about this all wrong. Maybe you should try to use some other skill."

She gave him a look. "It's stunning that you've known me this long and haven't figured out that I don't exactly have any awe-inspiring magical talents."

Thea could see Barris's contemplative expression and recalled her various attempts at fire, water, even at weapons training. Throwing knives had been particularly embarrassing.

He finally sighed, sinking into his own ready posture as he drew up his sword. "All right," he told her, "ready when you are."

They continued practicing stances, dodges, and striking techniques until her arms screamed for a break. She stretched her shoulders as Barris grabbed a canteen from near the fire. He tossed it to her then picked up a piece of leather, which Thea was fairly certain had been grown from a sapling into the shape of the seat near one of the benches.

"How's the collection going?" he asked.

She shook her head. "Still have three to go. We finished sorting the items Ruby had requested in her letter to the Council head, and I thought they'd be able to help with the list items as well, but Aster informed me I was wrong."

Barris smiled up at her in the dim light, clearly understanding that the girl had not done it kindly.

"Thornsblood, windroot, and king lily, and my mission is done."

Barris's brow drew down. "Never heard of those."

She shrugged, walking closer to inspect what he'd been fiddling with.

"Sword belt," he explained. He tied the last ribbon of leather then indicated to her waist. She raised her arms, and Barris leaned forward to wrap the belt at the proper height. He cinched the sheath with the belt, showing her how it should ride.

When he straightened, Thea glanced up to find Steed standing across the yard. Barris handed Thea her sword and followed her distracted gaze. It was dark night, likely nearing sunrise. She slid the sword into its sheath, her gaze returning to Barris to thank him for the work.

He patted her on the shoulder hard enough to knock her off balance, given the unusual weight at her hip. She chuckled. When Barris turned to go, Thea's gaze went back to the spot where she'd seen Steed, but he was gone. She stretched her shoulders again, wondered how the others possibly sat and slept with a bulky length of metal at their sides, and then realized with chagrin that she would be ahorse soon, and that would come with a whole new set of sword skills to master.

She turned back toward the barracks, ready to finally give in to rest. Thea froze at the sight of a dark figure at the edge of the trees. Her hand went for her short blade, then Steed's reminder raised its level head. *Call for backup. Warn the guard.*

Thea's mouth opened to shout, but the figure shifted, changing into something taller and narrower—something more fey.

The figure moved closer. "Oh," it said unpleasantly, "it's you."

Thea drew her blade. "Liana."

The changeling was dressed in green silks, her skin pale and pink, though Thea was certain it had been as dark as the night beneath the shadow of the trees a moment before.

Thea rolled her thumb over the handle of her dagger. "What do you want here?"

"Who," the changeling corrected.

Thea bit down her automatic reply, knowing her mouth would only get her into more trouble.

"Who?" someone asked behind her.

Thea didn't turn. She knew it was Steed at her back.

Liana's smile was only for him. "Summit," she purred, as if they were more acquainted than the two actually were. Thea had a flash of memory of Liana's hands trailing over Steed's bare chest. Her fingers tightened on her weapon.

"What are you doing here?" he asked Liana.

Liana spread her hands wide. "Trading favors, of course."

Thea felt Steed shift and his weapon going into its sheath as he moved to stand beside her. Liana came forward as well, swatting at a flittering pixie over her shoulder. The pixie was knocked sideways, shook itself, then flew away in a cloud of luminescent dust. "You know they won't abide you here," Steed said.

Liana ignored the warning, but she surely understood that. She'd come in the dead of the night, cloaked in shadow. The changeling leveled her gaze on Steed. "Trouble again, I'm afraid."

Thea felt Steed's posture go still beside her and the chill of fear thrill over her skin. "Tell me," Steed said.

"Ruby's gone onto fey lands in search of Pitt."

Liana was a changeling, a being who liked to toy with others and who enjoyed the chase and the game. For her to simply come out with such information meant they didn't have much time.

Thea looked at Steed beside her and watched his neck twitch in a swallow.

"I cannot go with you," Liana said, "but do make haste." Before Steed could turn away, Liana reached into her clothing and drew free a tightly bound scroll. "One more thing…"

Thea stared in disbelief as the changeling unrolled the very scroll she'd been given by Ruby, the list of supplies she was meant to gather on their journey. Liana held the document up and tapped the last item on the list.

"Thornsblood," Steed read.

Liana rolled the scroll tight once more, secured it with a ribbon of silk. "In your sister's own hand."

"I don't understand," Steed told her. "What does it mean?"

"Thornsblood is only available in one place," a voice from the darkness said. All eyes turned to Junnie as she emerged from the shadows with several Council warriors at her back.

Thea's voice was caught in her throat, but Steed managed a cold, "Where?"

Junnie's gaze narrowed on the changeling. "Beyond the last fey forest, where Isa waits."

11

FREY

BY THE TIME WE'D FINALLY RESOLVED THE ISSUES WITH THE rogues and made reparations, it was late in the day. Chevelle suggested we sup in his study, and after we'd finished eating, my boots propped up on a stool and my sigh heavy, he explained there was one more order of business. I sat up, leaning toward him as he retrieved a cloth bag from behind his desk and took the seat across from me. He slid the soft velvet back, revealing an ironwood staff.

My eyes left the intricately carved wood to meet his gaze. "I've been discussing with Rhys the ways in which his and his brother's powers are focused," Chevelle said, "and the way in which the fey first attempted to steal his own staff before they managed to break it."

I narrowed my gaze on Chevelle because I'd only just spoken to Rhys about his staff—Rhys had apparently neglected to mention he'd already discussed it with my Second at length.

"I'd like you to try this," Chevelle continued, "to see if it might help with your focus, to start."

At least he'd not explained that it was to protect innocent bystanders or so I didn't inadvertently blow anything up like before. It was a good idea, I supposed, and it might even work. Then I realized what he'd said. "To start?"

He drew the cloth fully away and lifted the staff toward me. "This one has been crafted as more than simply a way to focus your strikes and narrow your target. Inlaid into the crown is a stone from the ice lands." He shifted the end toward me, careful not to aim it in my direction. "It is a long shot, but I'll admit I have some hope it might work."

I examined the clear stone's uncut but polished surface. "Work for what?" I asked. The fey carried stones, not us. We didn't need to store power because we couldn't access it from a stone.

"We cannot draw from it," Chevelle said, answering my thought, "but it's possible you could still use it, were you to need a place to tie your power while fighting the fey."

Were he not there as my anchor, he meant. If I was alone. "You think I can tie to this stone?"

He shrugged one shoulder. "It is worth an attempt. Rhys does well with a staff, but Rider prefers none."

I reached out to run a fingertip over the carved ironwood, certain that it was not merely some simple attempt. Someone had spent many, many hours working on the weapon, and Chevelle clearly had far more than a mild hope that it would work. The wood was ancient—anyone could have seen that— but beneath my hand, I felt a strange sort of tingle, the way one might feel the warning of a spell.

I snatched my fingers back. "Tell me this isn't some sort of spellwork."

"No," he answered. "I knew you wouldn't touch it if the magic was tied to the earth."

My mouth turned down. "Darkness," I corrected. "Spellwork is tied to darkness."

He shook his head. "That's not the point. The staff is free of all castings. It's only a pure wood and a pure stone."

I reached out to touch it again, remembering the staff Asher had carried. He'd never let me—or anyone—touch it, though I wasn't sure why. I had always assumed he'd protected it against others, so that no one might steal something so valuable to him. I wondered if that was how he'd wielded so much power, all on his own. Or maybe it was only that he was much stronger than I was. My fingers brushed Chevelle's on the wood, and I pushed away the dark thoughts. "May I?"

He held the staff out for me, and I took it into my hands. It felt strange, cold, and something else that I could not quite understand. My questioning gaze met his again.

"There is a sort of energy of its own but only in that it needed to be powerful enough to hold your gift."

"And if I use it, if I tie my magic there?"

"There is no way to test it to be certain, but Rhys suggested it would be able to come back to you in the same way it flows between us." He straightened to stand, pressing his chair out of the way. "I don't recommend you try it here, but see how it feels and if it's a good fit."

I stepped into the space he'd made, holding the staff upright then shifting it as a weapon. It was light, its movements smooth, but there was a tangible weight to its energy, which seemed to meld with my own. I spun it around me once more then carefully returned it upright, base against the floor. "It's perfect," I told him.

He gave me a satisfied smile. There was something more to it, though, because it had suddenly become possible that I might be able to again stand on equal footing with the fey and avoid the gamble that one of a greater power—Veil, for instance—might be able to secure my magic as his own.

It was only for a time when Chevelle was not there as my anchor, I reminded myself. My own expression fell, and I felt my grip on the staff tighten. There was another danger I needed to plan for, one more possibility that needed to be laid out. Seasons before, I had named Chevelle my Second, but the truth was that if I fell, he was likely to go with me or follow shortly thereafter. It was what happened when elves were bound to one another—and the more powerful the elves, the stronger the bond.

My own ancestor had been overcome by it because she had been tied to Lord Asher.

The kingdom had only just regained its stability. I would need to name a true heir, someone to follow if Chevelle and I were both destroyed. The light caught on the stone atop my new staff, and I could not help but be reminded of the gift I'd received from Veil, twisted strands of silver and ice that were a warning of Asher's half-fey children, the ice of the fey not so different in appearance than the clear stone atop the staff. The gift from Veil had held two more strands as well, blood and bone. One represented me and one the half-human child, Isa.

Chevelle stepped closer, and I forced back the rumination. There would be time for that later. He'd just given me a gift of his own, which he clearly hoped would secure the very thing that held our kingdom together, its lord. "So," he said, "want to try it out?"

THEA

"Barris," Steed said to the waiting soldiers at Thea's back. She'd not even heard them approach, not with the roar of panic and dread in her ears. "Take the others the fastest route back to the castle. Warn Frey."

Barris gave a look in reply that Thea was fairly certain he shouldn't have given a superior, and Steed explained, "Duer will ride with me. I'll not be alone."

Thea's gaze flicked to Junnie and her warriors, and the Council head gave one curt nod. She would go, though Thea wasn't certain whether that was for Steed and the North or for the girl, Isa. Thea turned back when Barris grabbed her by the elbow. "Make haste," he ordered.

She glanced at Steed, who was tightening his weapons belt and calling for his horses. "No," she said. "Steed." His gaze flicked to hers only momentarily, but she willed him to stay focused on her. "She meant for me to go," Thea said. "Ruby gave me that list. Your sister said it was for me to do." When his mouth flattened into a thin line, she added, "She said, 'Steed cannot do this for me.' Do you remember?" Thea crossed her arms. "You were there. I am of the guard now. I do what they say." She tightened her own sword belt then, daring him to deny the order from another of the Seven.

Steed gave her a look but nodded Barris away. Thea felt the small squeeze Barris gave her elbow before he departed, and she managed to glance at him with no more than a bit of chagrin. He turned and ran, and each of the sentries was on horseback before she'd even settled her sword. Steed whistled, and their mounts, only just brought out by Junnie's men, moved toward them. Duer yanked Thea's bedroll free of her saddle then tossed the supplies she'd gathered for Ruby to the last of the sentries who were riding toward home. He was getting rid of dead weight, Thea realized.

She'd done it again. She'd leapt into a pit full of trouble without a single rope out. She closed her eyes tightly for one long moment then gripped her reins and jumped onto her horse.

They were off, riding into the trees before the rising of the sun. Shadows shifted behind those trees as they ran, and Thea knew it was wolves. Junnie was more than merely the head of a powerful Council of light elves. She was of the same blood as the Lord of the North and could draw beasts into action with no more than a thought.

The wolves were unnerving, but they made her feel more secure because where they were heading waited beings deadlier than a pack of wild animals. More feral, even. The fey lands had been brutal and terrifying. The fey were something else entirely.

She tightened her grip on the reins and leaned into the ride. It was too late to go back, too late but to face whatever fate would come.

13

RUBY

A SWARM OF PIXIES DROPPED RUBY UNCEREMONIOUSLY AT THE edge of the creek that bordered fey lands. She'd only just managed to jump to her feet when Willa was tossed from behind her, knocking them both over the edge and into the running water. A chill was in the predawn air. Ruby stood, gritting her teeth, and turned to glare at the cloud of dust and wings. The pixies tittered, jostling into one another as they parted from their swarm to disappear.

Willa stared up at them and blinked. Ruby grimaced, reaching down to pull the girl to her feet. "If you've not seen a pixie, you'll certainly not be interested in what waits at the other side."

The girl straightened and drew her sword.

It wouldn't matter, Ruby guessed. Likely, Willa would not be given a choice, given that she knew where Ruby was and what fey games were afoot. The sky was lightening. Ruby gave the girl one final look that asked, *Are you sure?*

The girl nodded, determined.

Ruby said, "Put your blade away. It'll do you no good."

When she did as instructed, Ruby gestured the girl to follow to the opposite edge of the creek. Ruby scanned the tree line and counted eight and ten high fey and at least a dozen sprites. There was a spike of orange across the horizon as the sun rose, and then the outline of a golden god appeared, his wings and arms spread wide.

Ruby rolled her eyes.

The girl beside her stared in wonder but not quite awe at the fey lord. Ruby could almost feel Willa's instincts to reach again for her sword. She didn't think she could blame her, as Ruby's own hand twitched in want of the whip. She'd been ready that time. Its barbs were tipped with a special blend of poison, just for the fey.

Veil's booted feet landed on the low grass of the creek bank, far enough back that it was clear the boundary was still in place. He was shirtless and golden, as always, but the fey lord wore a new arsenal of razor-sharp daggers. Those weapons did not shine in the glow of the morning sun like the man who wore them, because fey blades were not made of steel. They would be bone and wood, matter that did not cause their owner harm. It did not make them less deadly.

Veil's gaze struck Ruby, but before he could begin to preen, she demanded, "We have your protection?"

"Of course," Veil said. The announcement was not an order for Ruby and her guest but for those who waited in the trees.

Ruby nodded, stepping onto the creek bank beyond the protections of the ancient boundary and her own lands. Veil's attention moved to the girl behind her, and Ruby stepped between the two. "She's mine. She will stay mine. Any harm to her will be repaid tenfold to the beings responsible and to you personally."

Veil gave Ruby a look.

"I do not exaggerate," she told him.

"Fine." He gestured vaguely, but the shadows in the forest took note. The sun had fully risen, its glow illuminating the splendor that was the fey forest and the lord of its court. The season had shifted early, warming even the elven lands. It smelled of Veil, of summer winds and the bite of cardamom. Wide leaves shifted to let them pass, vines pulsing with the energy of that beneath the earth.

When they traveled farther into the forest, Ruby lengthened her stride to catch up. "You've found him, then?"

Veil glanced at her sidelong then back to the trees. "We should discuss this in my private quarters. Would you not agree?"

She glared up at him—she had no choice in the matter, given that she barely met his chest and couldn't fly. "We don't have time for this." His expression said he was in no hurry, so Ruby explained, "The others will notice we're gone soon."

The corner of Veil's mouth tipped into an odd angle, and Ruby's step faltered. "Not to worry, halfling," he said. "I've sent them a gift to occupy their time."

Heat flared in her palms, and Ruby hissed. Willa was beside her in an instant, sword drawn. Ruby shook her head and shoved the girl's blade down. "Will you stop that?" Her glare turned toward Veil. "We made a bargain. They are off-limits."

He spun to face her full-on, his wings flicking with irritation despite being drawn against his back. "No harm will come to any. You said nothing of distracting them."

"They've been through enough," Ruby said coldly. She did not trust his idea of distraction.

Veil leaned closer, his presence both overwhelming and enticing. "As have we all."

A wood nymph shifted in the trees, sprawling her body over a limb to stare down at them, and Ruby realized something about Veil she'd not before. Creatures had always been drawn to him—whether it was because of his access to the base magic or some inherent part of him, she wasn't sure, but they'd kept their distance. He wasn't being overrun as it was, but it seemed that a shift in his ability to move freely had occurred. She understood why. The heliotropes who had acted as his guard had kept the others at bay. Their power to sway the minds of anyone within reach and even cause a sort of hypnotism in weaker minds had allowed them to keep Veil safe without so much as lifting a sword. It was not the same power as Frey's. It wasn't an occupation inside their minds but more of an influence, a push.

It was enough. The heliotropes had been at Veil's side for as long as she could remember, and they had known him better than anyone. It was that familiarity that had cost him in the end, because they had betrayed him.

Veil might have been bitter about the entire ordeal, but Frey had stepped in to save him and hadn't truly betrayed their understanding, either. Frey had done what Veil had asked of her in the bargain, even if it didn't transpire in exactly the way he might have planned. She'd been smart not to let him step down from a fight with Pitt, because Pitt would have betrayed his word to her, as he'd done to Veil. It had nearly been a disaster, but in the end, the fey lord had gotten what he'd asked for, no matter if it was what he wanted. Anyone could expect as much from a fey trade, though Ruby reckoned a high fey lord did not usually give away the upper hand. Then again, he hadn't had much of a choice.

Veil walked through a particularly dense section of forest then brought them out to a wide clearing scattered with pale-gray stones. The morning sun shone brightly, a reminder of the stark darkness beneath the canopy from which they'd just emerged. Willa gave a little shake as she sidled up beside Ruby, apparently knocking loose phantom nightbugs. The fey lord glanced around the clearing, though the gesture was too smooth to appear anxious, then made a strange sort of call into the sky. It was not a sound as much as a feeling—the strong current beneath the ground purled and hissed in response, and though Ruby could not reach it, she could sense the movement as it flowed through Veil and around them. Willa must have felt it too or at least sensed something else, because her eyes rose with Ruby's to stare into the cloudless blue sky.

Ruby lifted a hand to shield her gaze as two dark masses swept past. A strange noise came from beside her, and Ruby glanced over to see Willa's mouth pop open in astonishment. Ruby's arm dropped to her side as she gave Veil a look, not at all surprised to find him wearing a ridiculously pompous grin. "How in the name of the realm have you managed to keep these a secret?" she asked.

"Secrets are our specialty," he purred.

Ruby blinked. "But *why* keep them hidden?"

His expression said that much was obvious. She didn't suppose he was wrong. After all, that was why he was bringing the animals there. Ruby—like the other elves—could not fly. The fey had the upper hand there.

She frowned, a hand twitching toward the barbed whip on her hip.

Veil's grin widened, and he lifted a palm as if he himself were guiding the glorious winged beasts to the ground.

Willa's voice was as light as a whisper beside them. "Those horses have wings."

Ruby pressed her fingers tightly into her palms. "I hope it was not a mistake to bring you along, soldier."

Willa's eyes cleared at the word, as steady and sure as ever as they met Ruby's.

Ruby nodded. "Excellent. Then let us ride these winged beasts into certain danger beside a high fey lord, shall we?"

Willa, who was usually nearly as solemn as Chevelle, grinned like an absolute charm. Ruby's head fell back in a laugh, and the horses eyed her as they alighted on the flattened ground of the clearing. If Ruby wished for anything outside of the success of her mission, it was that her brother could see them.

The beasts were massive and steel gray, muscled more thickly than any of Steed's best stock. Their wings were not those of the fey but more like a bird's, soft and structured and folding into and out of themselves with breathtaking ease. *This,* Ruby thought, *was where the fey obsession had stemmed from.* "How many are out there?" she asked.

Veil shook his head. "Few, and less every season."

"Because of the base magic?"

"The encroachment," he said. "Their lands were on the cliffs far past these forests. We saved what we could." The tilt of his brow said he'd seen it himself and that more than just these winged beasts had been lost.

"We need to go," Ruby told him. It was not meant as a reminder, because the fey lord knew the dangers better than anyone, but as a promise that it would be dealt with and the devastation would stop. They would find a way.

Veil's feet lifted barely off the ground as he swooped forward, spinning past Ruby to grab Willa by the weapons straps crossing her back. To her credit, she did not scream as she was hoisted into the air, but when Ruby vaulted herself onto the back of the opposite horse, she could see the girl's hands trembling. Ruby leaned forward, gripping the beast's mane, and pressed her knees and calves into the animal's sides and away from its wings. The girl watched carefully before doing the same. She nodded once to Ruby, who glanced at

Veil. He grinned again, though Ruby could not tell whether it was because of the sight of the two on horseback or in anticipation of what was to come.

Veil's wings took one long draw, and he rose into the sky above them. Ruby tightened her grip and made a silent wish, and the horse's entire being seemed to shudder beneath her before its body rolled up into an arc, its wings rising into a full spread to push the air beneath it. Ruby held her breath. It was not the flight of the fey—magic didn't drive the thing's motion. It was the sheer force of air and muscle, feather and bone. The beast's hooves left the ground, and its wings met, battering Ruby between the soft plumage and spikes of hollow bone. She ducked, not wanting to be pulled free, and they rose incrementally until they were fully airborne, driving upward and into that blue sky. She wanted to close her eyes, but the fey were watching. Despite everything that had happened, there was still one rule that could never be forgotten: one did not show fear to the fey.

She thought of attempting a glance back at Willa but could only take in the expanse of wing and sky. The beast tilted, and Ruby leaned harder into its back, twining her fingers more tightly into the animal's thick mane.

As they keeled sideways, Ruby could see the deep green of the trees below. The fey lands were massive, with forests as far as the eye could see. There were small breaks and clearings, and the stone formations held soft angles and light colors so unlike the jagged dark rocks of home. And there were towers and dwellings rising from the ground, though most fey lived and slept beneath the canopy of trees. The dark night in the forest was not a place Ruby ever wanted to see again, but the fey thrived there. It was home not just to Veil and his court but to countless beings who subsisted on the river of energy that flowed beneath its ground.

They finally reached the edge of that river of energy late into the day, where the creeping deadness could be felt even high in the air. The earth was dry, the ground packed, and the green going more than simply sparse—it turned to dust and withering leaves.

Veil dove closer to the earth, and Ruby understood that he would not cross that boundary. He would not step onto the barren ground, would not soar over land that was somehow being drained of the energy flowing through him.

It might have been superstition on the part of the fey. It was impossible to know if the deadening of that energy could at some point affect them beyond the draw on the base magic, but it was wise not to be the one who found out. The horses dove behind Veil, but when they neared the earth, they bucked and tossed their heads. Ruby leapt to standing, prepared to jump free, but Willa was thrown from her mount. Veil caught her a breath before she smacked into the ground, swinging her up to stand with a wince—Willa's petite form was laden with metal weapons. When they were at a safe height, Ruby jumped down, and the horses immediately took back to the sky.

Ruby straightened to dust herself off, and Willa took a small step away from Veil.

"This is where I leave you," he said. "I have men standing guard, but none will follow onto the encroachment."

Ruby narrowed her gaze on him. When Pitt had brought her to the edge of the barren ground to test her strength, there had been a pile of bones marking the land. And before that, someone had taken humans to the boundary between lands that the ancients had laid in place after the fey war. "Then how are they getting across?"

"I did not say no one crossed before. I said no one will follow now."

So not because of the humans. Ruby wondered what, then, was stopping them from crossing, and if it was Isa. Ruby remembered how they'd reacted to her before, how none of the fey had been interested in trying her, even among the fervor of the fates' dance. But there had been wolves, too, a horde of them. "And you think Pitt's there," Ruby said, "with the humans?"

"We have searched everywhere else. If he is not there, he is not within reach."

"You dragged me all the way out here on a suspicion."

The corner of his mouth twitched. "I did not."

That was it, then, all he was willing to give her. She supposed it was more than she would have had on her own.

Ruby felt Willa tense beside her and followed the girl's gaze into the low trees and sparse growth on the barren ground. Looking back at her were a dozen pairs of golden eyes.

"Perfect," she said to Veil. "A pack of wolves to replace you."

14

RUBY

RUBY STEPPED FROM THE FEY LANDS ONTO THE BARREN GROUND and felt the hollowness beneath it. There was a lack of something not quite tangible and the absence of the base magic's flow. In its place was a deadness, a stillness, and a pack of black-and-silver wolves. Ruby glanced at Willa, who appeared far calmer when faced with wolves than with fey, then moved to walk through the beasts and the trees ahead. Ruby knew she smelled of fey, but whether it was the scent of elves that kept her safe or that the animals had been given a long-ago direction against hurting her, specifically, she could not know. Because Ruby was certain the animals had been ordered to tear apart any fey that came near Isa.

The trees were short and thin, nothing like the forests of the fey. The growth was wild and tangled, not guided by magic or manicured in any way. Willa pulled a short blade from her belt, slashing at vines here and there. It was something she'd not attempted in the fey forests, which meant she'd been trained in more than how to deal with a blade. She knew something of the fey.

"What do you know of the humans?" Ruby asked her.

"Only the stories."

She meant rumors. She wouldn't have heard the tales from the fey, only accounts told by the elves who had gone to fight on fey lands beside the Seven, rogues and clans, the people of Camber.

The girl kept her gaze on Ruby, waiting.

"They are not dangerous," Ruby told her, though the statement felt wrong. The humans had a been a large part of the incitements of the massacre of the North, and the hollow ground beneath their feet spoke of something even darker. "It is not the humans we have to be careful of this time." It was the changeling who posed the threat to their lives. What he might look like when they found him, though, she didn't precisely know. "Nevertheless, keep your hand to your blade and your senses on alert."

Ruby didn't think she needed to remind the girl, because Willa had been on high alert since she was a child. The Lord of the North might not have been able to keep a close eye on each of her guard, but in her stead, Edan had. The head of the guard had started his watch before anyone set foot onto castle grounds, while they were still young and learning, and those with the gift of fire had been brought to Ruby's attention long before she had been asked to step in as trainer. If the Seven were to trust anyone to get that close to Freya, they would have been certain of the prospect's fealty first.

Ruby and Willa traveled far into the outer lands through forests and plains, the warmth of the day becoming more noticeable as they gained distance from the fey lands. The ground grew less fertile, dry and dusty in paths and patches, as if the land was not merely empty of the base energy but drained of the nutrients required to grow. Ruby couldn't be certain, though, because she wasn't convinced she'd ever seen land not tended at least in part by the hand of an elf or fey. They couldn't seem to help themselves.

When dusk finally started to settle, the shadows in the trees returned. The greenery was less imposing there, but there was no question what the beasts behind them were. The wolves came in closer, darting carelessly between the brush, dancing among their packmates. They were not the movements of beasts under sway. They were wild animals, likely brought there by Junnie but free of her command. There was the snap of a low limb and a strange whine. One shadow tumbled over another.

"Climb." Ruby's word was curt, her tone clear, and as she leapt into the branches overhead, swinging herself higher into the sparse canopy, Willa scrambled up behind her. The girl was capable enough, but the trees were not made for climbing. Their bark was smooth and slick, their limbs too few and far between. Were they to try to stay above ground, they would have a devil of a time getting from one to the next, but that didn't mean she was ready to take back to the earth.

Willa finally reached a limb near Ruby, and together they watched the shadows below. If they had to, they could fight the beasts, but Junnie had left them for a reason—and feral wolves were hugely preferable to a pack of wild fey.

Ruby leaned back to glance at Willa. The girl's hands were wrapped tightly around one branch, her feet perched on another. "Do you need to rest?" Ruby asked.

The girl looked up from the forest floor and shook her head.

"It can't be much farther." Ruby had been keeping track and knew how long it took the sentries to get in and out, unless Isa had moved the humans back even more.

She heard footfalls.

Willa went still a heartbeat after Ruby, though whether

she'd heard it herself or only reacted to Ruby was hard to say. Ruby held up a finger to indicate *wait here*, and when she received a nod, Ruby leapt from the branch into a nearby tree, springing as lightly as she could manage. The limb that caught her was too thin and bounced with her weight, shaking its leaves. She held her breath and clambered closer to the stem. It was too late. The footfalls had halted. She heard the whisper of a drawn bow.

They were Junnie's men, then.

"Cease," she said, dropping from the bough to the flat earth beneath. The wolves shifted and whined but did not move closer.

A tall woman in brown leathers and a thin green cloak stepped forward. Ruby lit a fire in her hands, raising it enough that the woman could see her face. The sentry lowered her weapon. "Are you an envoy from the North?"

Ruby doused her flame. "Something like that."

Two more sentries, a wiry male and a petite female with a crown of braids, moved from behind the trees.

"Come, then," the first one said. "Bring the girl too."

Ruby frowned, glancing over her shoulder to see nothing but forest and darkness. She shrugged, and Willa dropped from the tree with far less grace than Ruby had managed.

They walked much farther into the woods, and Willa took a long draw from her canteen before unclasping the neck of her vest and surreptitiously dousing her skin. It was warm, but Ruby kept forgetting that the fey part of her saved her from feeling overly uncomfortable. They came through the edge of trees soon, though, and in that last clearing waited a town the size of Camber.

Houses made from limb and stone dotted the open space, their roofs thatch, doors canvas. Primitive as it was, it was more than Ruby expected. They walked not through the houses but around the edge, where small fires glowed within stone pits at scattered intervals. The people were not hiding. Their settlement was no longer a secret. The fey and the Council wanted to know where the humans were at all times. They wanted to be able to find and track both the encroachment and Isa.

Willa's gaze darted over the structures, past the fires. She'd not seemed to disregard Ruby's words, but Ruby wasn't certain the girl entirely trusted that the humans were not a danger.

Their feet suddenly met thick grass where the dusty path of the settlement ended, the lush green a stark reminder of the contrast. Thin saplings rose in braided patterns to border the area, looking decorative by outward appearance but by purpose more of a fence. They walked through the gateway, arched overhead and latticed with vines, and saw ahead the low, wide wooden structure that was Isa's place.

Two sentries stood at either side of the building's doorway, pikes in hand. A third came out of the darkness, and the party of elves around them stilled, their arms going toward their chests in some sort of salute. Ruby gave a sidelong glance at Willa, whose downturned mouth said she'd noticed it too.

The newcomer said, "Put them in the bunker until dawn."

Ruby's hand itched for her whip. She said levelly, "Need I remind you to whom you're speaking?"

The sentry stared back, unflinching, the flickering firelight the only movement on his face. "The order was meant as a direction to my own men. I've neither the capacity nor the desire to direct one of the Seven."

"Nor the hospitality, it seems."

The sentry's eyes flashed, caught for an instant in the light. "It is not my place to offer hospitality. It is my place, however, to ensure the security of visitors until they might be seen."

Ruby tapped a finger against her leg. The sentry's gaze didn't follow it, as if he didn't think she was a threat. The female sentry who'd brought them in explained, "She sleeps until dawn. No one is to disturb her there, per the head of Council."

"Thank you," Ruby said to the woman. "We could use the rest as well." It wasn't true. She wanted to get to work right away, but there was something happening that Ruby did not understand, and she didn't like being caught off guard.

The female sentry turned without another word to the others, leading Ruby and Willa to a nearby structure built into the earth, its sides mounded with dirt. Ruby could smell the sulfur of spellcasting around it. "I'm not going in there."

The sentry said, "Protections have been placed on the structure. It is the only safe place on the premise."

Aside from Isa's residence, Ruby thought. She leaned close to the woman and kept her voice low. "What, exactly, are you protecting us from?"

The woman's mouth went into a hard line.

"That's what I thought." Ruby crossed her arms. "We'll fend for ourselves unless you're willing to offer information."

The woman shifted, the glance over her shoulder entirely casual by all outward appearance, and said, "Take to the trees."

Ruby gave one curt nod. "Call to me the moment she wakes. I've no time for waiting."

When they were again alone, Ruby led Willa into the thin trees that bordered the settlement. She felt for any sense of spellcasting, for any warnings of danger within the copse, and then chose a low-branched, sturdy tree, urging Willa to climb as high as possible while she went for supplies. It was only a moment before Ruby was caught again by the sentries, so she requested a bit of canvas and rope. She returned to the trees, climbing high to secure the girl into a makeshift hammock for the night. "Rest," Ruby told her.

The girl didn't look as if she could actually sleep, not in that strange place and so near humans, but she climbed carefully into the hammock anyway. Ruby waited beside her, watching the movement of the sentries and the shadows of the fire through a break in the trees. She would have to discover what she could during the night, because Junnie had left enough sentries behind that there would be no covert actions in the light of day.

Veil had assured Ruby that no fey would follow them in, so if the settlement had a reason to set protections, something else was in play. She checked on the girl one final time—she was too still to be sleeping, but her eyes were closed and her breathing steady—and leapt onto a nearby limb. She made her way through the tangle of forest toward the settlement, close enough that she could hear the crackle of fire over the chirp of crickets. He had to have been there somewhere. Pitt would not isolate himself in the barren lands for long. She swung herself onto another branch, moved closer, and peered over the settlement's rooftops. A wind picked up, blowing the scent of smoke and the earthiness of the humans toward her. The clouds parted, lighting the scene with the soft silver light of the moon.

There must have been twenty sentries patrolling the settlement, which meant there would be two additional shifts of patrols during the daylight hours, plus those sentries who roamed the woods and boundaries. Junnie had sent new reinforcements, but it seemed not all of her initial group of guards had gone back home. Ruby waited for the sentries to pass, but they were smart enough not to take their routes in an obvious pattern. Only a few repeated their movements, while the rest scattered and wandered and watched where they might. She climbed down slowly, hiding behind the trunk of the narrow tree for a moment before creeping closer to the nearest structure.

She reached out, brushing a hand over the timbers that made up its walls, pressing her fingertips between them to climb onto the roof's edge. She might have been small, but Ruby wouldn't risk climbing the thatch. It appeared to be sturdy, but she couldn't know if it had truly been made by elven hands. She waited for another sentry to pass then shifted to drop into the opening that made a doorway. Her boots were silent on the packed earth, her eyes not taking long to adjust to the lack of light.

Three cots lined the outer wall of a single open space, with two humans in each and a small child at the foot of one. There were pots and containers on a low, wide table and a few garments draped over a peg in the wall. Oil lanterns sat on a stone tablet by the doorway, their wicks blackened and the metal cold. The room smelled of onion and musk. Two basins and a pitcher rested on the floor beneath the table. A pair of stools, one draped with leatherwork and needle, centered the room. The child stirred, flopping a leg free of its bedding before settling again. Its chubby little fingers curled into the fur of a pelt.

She knew there would be a garden nearby and livestock. And despite the dirt surrounding the settlement, the humans seemed relatively clean, so there had to be a good water source.

Pitt would not have stayed near the running water. She peered out the canvas doorway and scanned the seemingly endless array of structures. If her information was correct, Isa was at the settlement of humans nearest the border. Beyond there would be countless more settlements containing an unmanageable number of humans. Junnie's sentries were guarding the border and Isa, but the others were merely being held back from the fey by Isa's command—by her talent to slip into their minds.

Ruby suspected that Isa and her men would have created some sort of order, that the humans under Isa's watch would be told how to direct the others, and word would spread. The salute she'd seen between the sentries suggested something more military than she might have felt comfortable with, but she was unfamiliar with how the humans responded to being managed by magical beings.

She waited for a break in the sentries before darting back into the trees. She took a quick glance at the girl's hammock then moved again, following the settlement to the edge of the woods. From there, she could see dark, flat, tilled earth and beside it, patches of green in broken rows. A garden—she could smell it. Ruby leapt to the ground, running toward the plots of land only to freeze suddenly when she recognized a dark shape as that of a child kneeling before the soil.

She heard the whisper of a drawn bow, echoed by three more.

15

FREY

"You have got to be kidding," I said.

Chevelle's mouth was a hard line. He wasn't kidding.

He had reported another incident, which made one too many to be mere chance. I stood, sword still in hand, and he gestured for Kieran to bring in the next three clan leaders. Two were covered in blood, the last wearing a fur mantle that had clearly been singed. "What is it?" I asked flatly.

The clan leader—who I'd only just realized had not been announced—in the burned mantle said, "Rogues attacked our stock, drove our horses into imp territory, and set fire to our stores." I waited for more information because the complaint was never the end of the story. At my silence, he added, "When we tracked them back to their camp to demand recompense, they denied the accusations and attacked our men."

"What quarrel would they have with you?" Chevelle asked.

The clan leader opened his mouth to respond but fell silent.

"None," Chevelle answered for him, "and yet you were able to track them back to their camp."

The clan leader shifted, evidently not clear on what my Second was implying.

"This is the fifth attack in so many hours," Chevelle told them. "Gather a summit. Send word when you have it set."

The man nodded, backing away with the others.

Chevelle looked at me, his expression flat. "I'll send word to Anvil to attend their summit. Rhys and Rider can accompany me to meet with the rogues."

"It's nearly sunup," I told him. "Surely, it can wait until dawn."

The twist at the edge of his lips reminded me that we'd fielded half a dozen reports of incidents since late afternoon, and it didn't seem as if it was going to slow down. I sighed. "All right. I'll go with you to tell them. I want to see if they've made progress before they're called away."

We walked the dim corridors, nearly empty of staff and guards, toward the study. Ena had tried to serve us dinner hours before, but she'd given up, resigned to accepting our refusal. I was too exhausted to eat after the day we'd had, in any case. Chevelle's hand brushed my back as a reminder to turn not toward our rooms but the study.

We passed through the arched stone doorway to find Rhys and Rider still working, despite it being well into the night. It often felt as if I was the only one who required regular sleep to stay focused, which was apparently a product of my human heritage. Based on the shifting stack of ledgers, it seemed they had made progress. They both made to stand, but I waved them off. "What have you found?"

A large map was spread over the table between them, two stone sculptures shaped into hawks holding down its edges. "Studying the lay of the land," Rhys answered. He gestured toward the ice lands, much of them uncharted on our own maps, and ran a finger toward the fey forest and its outer boundaries. "Looking for some connection to the waterways or mountains."

"You think the base magic runs that far?"

Rider shook his head. "No, but something deeper might."

Rhys slid a manuscript toward us, its cover showing clear evidence that it was ancient. "There are legends in our lands not so dissimilar from your own."

Chevelle leaned forward to take the manuscript. He held it carefully, examining the cover. "Where did you find this?"

"We've been given access to the vault and Asher's personal rooms."

"Have you seen it before?" I asked.

Chevelle's gaze met mine. "No."

"But there's something unusual about it?"

He held the book forward, showing me the design. I took it, sitting numbly in a chair, unable even to trace the etching with a fingertip.

The cover was oiled leather, held in place by metal studs. Carved into its center stood a pair of crudely outlined figures, neither clearly male nor female. Around them were lines of symbols, and above them, a pair of wolves.

I stared up at Chevelle then looked to Rhys and Rider.

"It is an uncredited account," Rider explained. "We've no idea who is responsible for it or how much has in fact been proven true."

"And yet…"

"And yet," Rider answered, "there appears to be some correlation to what has happened to Finn and Keaton and what holds the boundaries between lands."

The wolves had been present the whole of my life—since before my mother had been destroyed and I'd been bound—

but their story was only legend. The wolves themselves could not tell it, so what remained were tales passed down from those who had witnessed their transformation, men who had long since passed into nothing. "You think this is connected?"

Rhys laid down the parchment he'd been holding. "If it isn't, it's a step at least in the right direction. Inside that manuscript is the only written record of their… transmutation. And in that same manuscript, the methods by which the fey can be controlled."

Rhys looked up, and I turned to see Kieran at the doorway. He did not look as if he expected to be well received. I bit back a growl. "More rogues?"

"Yes," he answered. "This time, closer to Camber."

I felt Chevelle straighten beside me, his attention drawn from the manuscript. Anvil and his men were near Camber, so surely the rogues would not be so brazen or foolish.

Kieran's gaze left us as he glanced down the corridor, and then he stepped aside, still standing at attention. After a moment, Grey entered the room, slightly pale and with a bit of sway to his step. Chevelle met him halfway across the space, taking him by the arm to steady him. "What is it?"

"I…" Grey started, putting a hand to his temple. "I must have fallen asleep." He shook his head, apparently clearing whatever he'd been thinking, and said, more urgently, "Ruby. Has anyone seen Ruby?"

The room went silent, with not a single affirmation or move.

Grey looked sick. "She hasn't been in. Not even to minister to my wounds."

All eyes fell to me at the sound of my chair sliding across the stone floor. I stood, waiting for the news I did not want to hear. "How long?"

"I'm—it's a little fuzzy, but late afternoon?"

It was nearly dawn.

Chevelle snapped my name, and I tamped back the rage that swam through the room. My magic was still too volatile, and I could not let it move freely. I had to remember to hold my temper in its place.

"When did you sleep?"

Grey shook his head, immediately understanding the accusation. "She didn't drug me. If I was—" His words fell off, because of course he'd been drugged. He hesitated and seemed to taste his tongue. "It was the fey."

Early afternoon. Drugged by the fey. "They've had too much time. She's already there."

We'd been played the fool because we'd fallen for the distraction, the false battles between the rogues and clans set up by fey.

I wondered what we would do. We would certainly chase after her again, despite what it had cost us the last time.

But Keane was gone, the fates' dance over. So it was something else—Veil or worse.

"Pitt," Grey said.

"She would have never found him," Chevelle replied.

"That wouldn't stop her from trying." Grey ran a hand over his face, and Rider stood to bring the man water.

"How would they have gotten into your rooms? Ruby has protected you more severely than any—" Rider's words fell off as he realized the truth of what he'd said, as he understood his own accusation.

Ruby was in on it.

Ruby had not been taken by the fey. She'd gone willingly.

16

RUBY

RUBY STOOD STOCK-STILL, WAITING FOR THE RELEASE OF THEIR arrows. But the girl put up a hand, not bothering to turn from her task. "Let her be," she said, pressing her nimble into the soil of her garden again.

Ruby glanced at the sentries, letting her disapproval at being threatened as an envoy of the Lord of the North show, though she couldn't be certain precisely how much longer that ruse might stand. She moved toward the girl, and Isa lit the lantern beside her. It cast light over her small hands, which were covered in dark, fertile soil. She frowned up at Ruby. "I can't get these to grow."

Ruby leaned down to examine the plants, their roots dark and wilting. "Not a species that would do well here, I'm afraid."

Two more lanterns lit behind her, and Ruby realized they'd been lit not by the girl but by her guard—so she'd been in the dark before, apparently hiding what she'd been doing. Her petite face rose to show Ruby her expression, a frown that said she'd been raised by people who could make anything grow anywhere. Ruby looked for the sentries, but they were moving away at some unseen signal that the girl was safe or no longer wanted them to hover.

Ruby knelt beside the girl. "You understand that the magic is different." Light elves had magic that excelled at making things grow, but that talent was not as well suited to the dark energy of the North. Isa was of Asher's line, not Junnie's. She would be good at other things.

Isa brushed the dirt off her palms. "I'm not a fool." She gestured to the garden plots before them, a variety of vegetables that would more than sustain a settlement this size. "It's not just me," Isa said. "The others cannot grow here either, not as they did on our own lands. We are limited by the soil and limited by the sun and limited by whatever energy we can provide."

"So why this, then? What's so important about having more than what is clearly thriving?"

The girl placed the wilting plant onto Ruby's palm. Her eyes were wide, their green unnaturally dark in the lantern light. "It's not merely in this garden," she explained. "We cannot grow here, not even in the potted soil inside my study. Not even from earth brought in from home."

Ruby felt the strangeness of the plant she was holding, the hollowness of it, which was so faint that she might not have noticed without the girl's explanation. So this earth, or whatever the humans brought to it, was turning the energy somehow, and it went beyond what lay beneath fey ground. "How far out have the scouts gone now?" She couldn't help but wonder the distance to which the humans' effect had spread.

The girl shook her head. "As far as any have gone, all is the same."

"And the others, those who have stayed in the settlement

long-term?" Ruby let the question hang, not wanting to voice her concern, not wanting to ask whether it had taken something from the energy inside the elves who were posted there, protecting Isa.

Isa glanced past Ruby into the darkness. "Not that I've seen," she said, but her tone made it clear it was only a matter of time. She sighed. "The dampening feels broader than any of us expected. I fear the fey have not given us their full understanding of the matter." She took the plant back from Ruby's hand and laid it reverently in a pile with the others. "But you're not here for any of that, are you?"

Ruby leaned her weight onto her heels, the posture putting the two at eye level as they knelt beside the garden. Isa had grown, she realized, again seeming older than her years. Ruby suspected that was all for the better, because they'd settled a responsibility upon her that would require a level head. "No," she said. "I'm here for the changeling, Pitt."

Isa nodded. "Junnie has set protections to deter him as well, though I doubt he will gain much from any of us." With her chin up, the girl looked so much like Frey—not the lord Frey had become, but the girl she was before, broken and bound—that it was painful. "It's not as if he'd destroy me here. Not until he's got what he needs to survive."

Ruby set her jaw. She'd been afraid of that, afraid they all knew he was still a threat and that he would return to destroy what was left the moment he had a way to live long-term without the base power. And they'd kept it from her, kept her hidden within the castle walls while they sorted out what to do. "The only thing keeping him alive now is that stone." Her ruby, the one he'd stolen from her, the one that had belonged to Frey's family. No one knew Asher had altered it.

Ruby's gaze met the girl's, full on. "Where do I find him?"

"I cannot tell you where, but once you do find him, I can tell you for certain that it is him."

Ruby knew that because Isa could feel the minds of humans, she would be able to feel that Pitt was not human, even if he hid among them. She could not control the fey, and the changeling, above all else, was wholly fey.

17

THEA

THEA HELD THE REINS TIGHTLY AS THEY SPED THROUGH THE shallow water bordering the fey lands. They'd gone in south of the usual crossing, as the ancient wolves, Finn and Keaton, had apparently given Junnie new access. Thea wasn't certain the others had been aware of the new crossing, but Steed had held his reaction close to the vest, so she hadn't the clues to properly decide.

Not that it mattered. Other things had been on her mind since their sprint from the village, like the fact that they were heading right back into fey lands—the very place where they'd nearly been killed such a short time ago. She forced a steadying breath, wondering if Barris and the others had made it back to the castle. It wasn't likely. They were probably only just nearing Camber.

The horses darted into the forest, heedless of the low limbs and thick brush. They should have left the animals at the border, Thea knew, but there hadn't seemed to be time. She ducked out of the way of a tangled vine, keeping her head low and trusting her horse to use his own head well. Thea remembered the forests from their last trip, and she knew the path was kept clear. She felt something akin to the tingle of a cast spell and could see more than simply foliage ahead. She'd no doubt that the path was used often by Junnie's men but also sensed that the men had kept it clear for their use. She could only hope they'd protected it from fey attacks as well. She suddenly remembered the wound on Steed's chest, the shredded meat of his side. Liana had healed him, but the cut from the poisoned blade had been meant to end him and nearly had.

Thea glanced at Steed as he rode, leaning forward with his hands pressed to rein and horse. Steed had never been a coward, but he had sense. He'd been cautious any time the situation called for it. This situation *screamed* for caution, though Thea understood why he'd none to give. Ruby was his sister, even if it was only by half. She was the only family he had left.

Steed's father had left after Ruby was born. When the venom in Ruby had killed her fey mother, their father had been released from the woman's thrall. He was still alive, but living did not make him a man. The elves were steady beings, not prone to fits and flights of fancy like the fey were. But when one fell too far into grief or rage, they did not always come back. That was where Steed's father lived now, over that edge of sanity, from where there was no return. There was only Ruby to call Steed's by name and by blood.

"Arms in," a voice shouted from the front, and Thea jerked just in time to shave by sharpened pikes of glass.

The fey had laid traps, it seemed. Thea stayed down, glancing over her shoulder to the horses and riders behind her. Two sat straight, holding bow and blade, with the others hidden by the mass of leaves and brush on the curving path.

THEY RODE THROUGH THE NIGHT, having crossed just after dawn. By the time they reached the encroachment, the sun was midday high.

Junnie's men met them at the border. The wolves who had led and followed during their run waited outside the tree line, just beyond fey land. The men wore cloaks of green and gold, their decorations simple, the material thin. All had light weapons and leathers, spears and knives, swords and bows. As a group, they charged toward the settlement, a small town of thatch-roofed houses and flat, dry ground. The soil was fair and dusty, not nearly rich enough to sustain the growth Thea had expected to see. At the edge of the makeshift town, they climbed from their horses, and Junnie's men took the animals to wipe them down and give them rest and food and drink. Thea suddenly worried about whether the water was safe or that of the fey, but she supposed if Junnie had left the girl there, there would be no danger to a horse.

Junnie was striding away from the group, headed toward a low structure on the outskirts of the cluster of homes. Steed and the others followed. Thea rushed to catch up, aware of the eyes of the local Council sentries on her. She and Steed stood out, their dark hair and clothes a manifestation of everything the light elves hated. She remembered Steed's attire when he'd been a trader, the brown of saddle leather and the common blades. He'd known how to fit in. He'd known how to keep from being a target. Steed's easy manner had gotten him far, but his ability to blend in went deeper than a jest and a smile.

She'd never felt so watched, even in the closeness of those fey trees.

The group came to a sudden stop, and she bumped into Steed's back, cursing silently for letting herself get caught in the stare of one of the sentries. Steed didn't turn but held steady as she shuffled beside him, at attention like a proper guard of the North. From inside the low structure came the half-human girl, Isa. Thea gaped at her, in awe of the way she'd changed. She was still scrawny with a mess of black hair, but she'd grown so much, aging at the rate of a fey rather than an elf. The girl's chin was stubborn, her shoulders straight. Her green eyes crossed over the rest of them before landing on Junnie, who was apparently her only real concern.

"My Isa," Junnie said.

The girl's smile transformed her face. She was suddenly a child again, not a strange, strong creature who seemed so in control of an entire population. Junnie moved forward to take Isa's hand, her urgency returned. "We are in search of the Summit girl, Ruby."

Steed did not react to the lack of her title, and Thea realized something else. Ruby had come not as one of the Seven— she'd come against the wishes of the Lord of the North. But Steed hadn't. His retrieval of his sister would be at the command of that same lord, spoken or not.

"She's gone," Isa said.

Steed flinched, and Thea had to resist the urge to take his hand and offer comfort. It was an uncomfortable response, one she should not have had, but she needed it as much for herself as for him. Ruby being gone meant that they would have to keep looking.

They would be going deeper into fey lands. Her stomach tightened.

"Where?" Junnie snapped.

Isa's expression was impassive, as if it did not matter to her, even though it clearly mattered much to the rest of them. "She's gone after the changeling, to secure her home and the lives of those she cares about."

Junnie said a very unpleasant word. "Does she have clues to where he might be?"

"No," Isa answered. "But should she find him, she will bring him here."

Why? Thea wanted to say, but she bit her tongue. It was not her place to ask questions, and she was trying her best to do right by her post and by Steed. Then she remembered what her post was, why she was there. She took a small step forward, not quite able to get her boots to stick a full stride with so many bright eyes on her.

The girl's gaze turned to her.

"Where can we find thornsblood?" Thea asked.

Isa's face split into a grin. "She's a clever one, then."

Thea understood she'd been speaking of Ruby and the fact that she'd left some sort of message or trail for them to follow. It did not make her feel better.

"Taryn," Isa snapped, the command less like that of Junnie and more like the leads in the guard. "Take them to the grove."

Junnie squeezed the girl's shoulder in farewell, giving her a long look, and Isa added, "Make haste. She's got a fair start on you. I will be waiting for your return so I might show you the gardens."

The shift in her tone, suddenly conversational, threw Thea's focus, but not for long. They were moving again, not on horseback but on foot, running straight for the trees across from the settlement as Isa's sentry led the way. Soon, they might find Ruby and, with her, a dangerous changeling fey who had nearly bested the high fey lord. Thea could not spare the room in her thoughts to focus on it, but if they made it out alive, she would have words with Ruby about the list and its task.

RUBY

RUBY STOOD ALONE AT THE EDGE OF A LINE OF POPLAR TREES, waiting for the coming darkness of the night. Her eyes scanned the trees, searching for any single thing out of place. She listened for sounds above the rustle of leaves in a gentle wind, wanting to acquaint herself with their whispers before the rise of the chittering nightbugs. That forest was new to her, the land occupied by an unfamiliar set of beasts and bugs. In the trees behind her waited Willa, the young sentry who would be guarding her back. It had been fortunate the fey had brought her along when they could just as easily have pushed her from the roof or dropped her along the way. Ruby was glad the plan had not yet cost her the lives of those she supported, and she hoped it would stay that way.

She would keep Willa secure from the changeling by distance. Ruby herself would be the only one she'd allow into the cursed being's path.

She waited longer, until the night went still. Ruby knew what that stillness meant. *This is it. It's time.*

She caught her gaze on the depthless eyes in the darkness, their shine like a bloodbeetle's shell. She let the fear she felt inside of her free then, allowing it to show openly on her face. She turned from the changeling, her prey. And Ruby, made of fire and will, venom and spite, *ran*.

THEA

THEY DID NOT FIND RUBY AT THE THICKET OF THORNSBLOOD trees. There had clearly been no one there at all. Junnie had let her trackers look anyway, let them scour the ground and the leaves and search for clues that Ruby might have left. They had gone farther into the forests and plains, searching for signs of her in all directions, but there was none.

When they finally rounded back near the settlement and Isa's home, Junnie suggested that they meet again with Isa, rest, and regroup. That was how Thea found herself in the small wooden barracks, half hidden beneath the earth and creeping with the tingle of fresh spellcasting. She sat beside Steed, the narrow room pushing them too close together, and stared at her feet as he sharpened a knife he'd pulled from his belt. He was busy thinking—she knew he was—but she couldn't seem to help herself. "Why did she say thornsblood if she was not going to be there?"

Steed was silent so long that Thea thought he'd decided not to answer. When he finally spoke, she jumped in the quiet stillness. He laid the blade aside. "She knew I would come for her the moment I found out." His eyes were dark in the dim light of the shelter, some of his concern hidden in their depths but some showing plainly. "The entire list was to occupy extra time so that I would still be gone when I received word." He pressed his lips. "She must not have known exactly when they would take her."

Thea felt her hand move toward him but stopped to roll her fingers over her palm. "Because she needed you with Junnie?"

He shook his head slowly. "Because if I were in reach of our commander, I would have been ordered not to go."

Thea thought of another of the Seven, Grey, pulled from his duties after he'd been injured and put under watch. Steed had nearly died at the hand of a fey. Her chest went tight, her breath coming in measured beats. "And you would do it anyway. You would have defied an order." Ruby had done the same, and Thea wondered what Ruby's punishment would be, given that she'd gone to such trouble to save her brother from it. "This way, you are not at fault."

He glanced down, running one palm over the other.

"But," she started, hating that she couldn't seem to let it be, "why me? Why not just send the list to Junnie and let you and the others figure it out?" Thea was only a new recruit, a guard with no stake in the strange game.

Steed's painfully intense gaze came back to meet hers. "If I were to become injured, you would be there to heal me."

Her eyes flicked to his side, where beneath layers of cloth and weapons waited that scar she'd stitched together time and again on their last ride into fey lands with Junnie. She wondered if he would be hurt again, if the fey would come after Steed because he was Ruby's flesh and blood and one of the Seven. Steed had gone still. Thea realized she was touching him, her hand on his thigh. She wasn't sure when she'd done it, but it was there, and she couldn't seem to gather the wits to pull it free. A sort of tension built between them, unspoken words and warnings they'd likely both heard before. It was not a safe thing. It was not smart, not a jump-into-it-headfirst sort of decision.

Her throat went dry, but she was moving for him anyway, drawing closer as if that hand was an anchor, the only thing keeping her from drifting away. Steed shifted but not farther from her, only straighter, and anything he might have said did not make it past his parted lips. She rose from the bench to meet his posture, the leather straps crossing her chest grazing his own. His hands came up to touch her arms, bare since she'd tossed her cloak at the door.

It might have been the wrong thing to do, but Thea wasn't certain her punishment wouldn't be worth it. She could see a hint of Steed's thoughts running over his face, but he did not appear to be weighing discipline either. He was probably thinking of his duties, of how easy it would be to tighten his grip and press her back to her seat before she crossed the line. But it was too late for that.

She eased closer, their breaths mingling as she brushed her lips over his with only the barest touch. He melted beneath her, the grasp on her arms turning into a soft caress. His thumbs ran over the delicate skin on the inside of her elbow, slowly up her biceps. She sighed, closing her eyes and kissing him again, softly and tenderly, mirroring the careful touch of his hands. His fingers trailed over her shoulder, the side of her neck. If he tugged her into him, she would be lost, and maybe they both knew it.

She opened her eyes to find him watching her with something like reverence in his gaze. She drew back to see him better, to gauge whether she'd gone too far. His fingers tensed against her as if he wanted to bring her back for more. She bit her lip in a smile then leaned in to nip at his.

There was the scuffle of movement outside, and Thea froze. Steed let out a breath, barely perceptible but a sign that he would much prefer to continue with her as opposed to something—maybe anything—else. She started to move away from him, certain she should quickly straighten back to her seat before they were caught, but he pulled her close for one more long, sweet kiss. For a moment, he held her gaze, and it seemed like a promise that this wasn't over.

Thea took a steadying breath and brushed her trembling hands over her clothes. She'd not been disheveled, though she certainly felt like it. She cleared her throat as Steed stood and slid his knife back into his belt. He glanced down at her as she tried to pull herself together. She managed a shrug. The corner of his mouth twitched, but he only turned, walked toward the door, and handed her her cloak as he ducked to leave.

She followed him out, draping the cloak over her arm as they stepped into the dark of night to meet Junnie and her guard.

FREY

I STOOD AT THE ANCIENT BORDER BETWEEN LANDS, LAID IN place long ago by our forebears and restored again by elves so powerful they'd gone not into death but into the minds of cunning beasts. Beside me stood my Second, and beyond him were four others of my Seven and a fair number of our guard.

None of it seemed to matter a whit to the high fey lord who waited on the other side of that boundary.

Veil relaxed into a high-backed chair, the seat not grown out of the earth but apparently brought in for just this occasion. He glanced over the tips of his fingers, examining them with far more care than he'd given any of us.

I pressed my eyes closed and took a steadying breath. Through clenched teeth, I hissed, "Veil," but the sudden flick of his gaze to mine—and what I saw in it—cut my threat short.

His mouth tipped up into a sly and scheming smile, and he purred, "We are no longer under treaty, my Freya."

My stomach turned at the honey in his voice, the reminder

of my words to him at court. I said, "You have broken this treaty. We intend to remain at peace—"

He *tsked* at me. Actually *tsked*, as if I were not the ruler of a kingdom as large as his own, as if I did not hold him trapped within that land, and as if he didn't need me to keep his people alive.

"Safe passage is my right," I said. "And as I alone control the encroachment that threatens your life and your land, I expect it done with haste."

"Demands, demands, demands," he mused. "And yet nothing in return." He dropped the hand he'd been examining to give me a level stare. "You and your Isa have done nothing toward repairing our lands and driving the scourge backward. Even now, she builds her encampment with gardens and stock, with housing made for permanence just outside our lands." He stood, leaning toward me. "On land that used to be ours. Land that once ran fertile with the base magic at the turn of the moon." Anger simmered beneath his words in a way I'd not seen in years. "And what of you, Lord Freya, in your castle on the hill?"

My mouth went dry. "We are working on the solution every moment of every day."

"There is one solution," he told me. "One to take it all away."

"Perhaps this is not the best time to discuss the situation," I seethed, "given that an urgent matter awaits on the other side of your lands."

"Let it wait," Veil spat.

"The changeling is a danger to both lands," Chevelle said. His voice was even and cold, and even if by Veil's estimation, my Second had spoken out of turn in a matter between lords, he could not fault the truth of it.

Veil glanced at me sidelong, his expression managing to

convey more than a few choice words of his own about Chevelle.

I crossed my arms. "Let us pass under invitation, or you shall come to regret it."

He turned to face me fully, stepping closer to the steady stream of water that trickled over stone. "Threats, then."

"I'll not bargain our way in." *Not again.*

Veil's wing flicked, no doubt in annoyance as he remembered our bargain, which had nearly cost him his life. "As if I would trust you to hold your word."

I tightened my hand around the grip of my sword. "Insult me again and see how far it gets you."

Veil's gaze flashed with something that might have been delight and might have been anger—it was impossible to tell when the fey reveled in both—and then slowly trailed toward Chevelle. Up, then down, up again as it came to rest about the height of my shoulder. I did not look because I knew what he saw. The staff that had been crafted for me. The one my Seven had insisted I not reveal was my own until and unless it was needed.

I didn't need it yet. I had Chevelle. With him and outside of fey lands, I had enough power to fight the high fey lord. Before, I had not been so lucky. Deprived of an anchor and exposed to Veil at his full power, I had been unable to risk setting my own magic free. But now, even though the base magic was flush with blood spilled during the fates' dance, it would be a fair fight.

And if he managed to separate me from Chevelle, I would pray the staff and its stone were strong enough to aid me. "Do you expect me stand here and watch you preen when we are needed beyond the border? To leave this threat to be resolved by only two of my Seven?"

Veil let me see the warm smile in his amber eyes. "Two of them?"

His tone questioned my certainty, and my chest bore a sudden icy stab of fear. Steed had to be with her. Anvil had met one of the guards in Camber before Barris found us on our path to the border. They had said Steed and Junnie had made their way to the fey lands. Both had assured us Ruby would not face the challenge alone.

If he had harmed any of them…

Veil chuckled at my expression, the threat plain on my face, and then brushed aside the matter with a flip of his hand. "It is of no consequence whether—"

"You are a vile plague," I hissed. "You never intended to let us cross because you've already made your bargain."

The fey lord's bronzed skin flushed with pleasure. He'd only been keeping us occupied while their plans played out, the same low tactic they'd used to keep us from realizing she had been gone. Fury rolled through me, agitating the power I barely had a hold on under normal circumstances.

Caught in his game or simply tired of waiting, Veil rose from the ground. "Until we meet again, my Freya."

Fire—mine—shot through the space between us, and his cackle echoed over my skin as he dodged the strike with his wings spread widely. He might have had cause to call out my attack, but he'd provoked me with his slithering, too-familiar tone, and he wanted to play. He threw me a wink before he turned, his golden figure disappearing into the tall trees.

I turned to Chevelle, who had the good sense to stare straight ahead and not back at me, and fumed. He and Ruby had made their bargains before I'd been restored to the throne. They'd done what they had to in order to get us all to where we were. But it was over.

"One more of you bargain with the fey, and I will personally see to your punishment," I said in a low tone, letting my gaze hit Chevelle, Anvil, Grey, Rhys, and Rider, every of my Seven in attendance.

THEA

Junnie looked agitated, and it wasn't merely because they'd not found Ruby, Thea thought, but because of something more. Steed watched her quietly, waiting for the words that would give him direction. Thea thought that the "something more" would not be spoken there, not with the eyes of so many upon them. Junnie flicked a finger at her side, and Thea saw the smear of what appeared to be soil or decomposing plants.

"The wolves are on alert. We need to go now," Junnie said.

Steed nodded. He'd been ready for nothing else.

"There are too many of them." Junnie had changed into slim pants and tall boots, her lean figure dressed to run and to fight. "I'm having trouble pinning down which area to strike first."

"We can split up," Steed started, but Junnie waved him off.

"This isn't merely her," she explained. "Something else has them rattled. We go as one." She snapped a gesture to her guard, and all came to attention, prepared for action and on alert. Junnie's gaze flickered, then, a sort of shuttering of her pupils, and Thea's stomach dipped at the realization that she'd been in the minds of those beasts.

She wondered how far Junnie could control them and how many at once.

Her palms sweated, and Thea ran them over the fabric at her hips, wanting to be ready if she needed to use her blade. It was nearing dawn, and soon, the humans would be rising from their slumber to fill the encampment with a different sort of activity, securing food and keeping shelter. Thea did not wish to be there when the settlement came to life. She did not wish for their wide, round eyes to be upon her.

That did not mean that she preferred to be so near the fey forests at night.

"Go." Junnie's directive to the waiting guard was clipped, her grave expression making her face seem sharp beneath her tight blond braids. Three of the women, the scouts who had been designated to search for danger, shot toward the trees. Junnie turned with the others to follow, with Steed at her back and Thea behind them.

As they entered the forest, a pack of wolves came with them, drawing nearer Junnie and her men from where they had been scattered and waiting. Junnie was powerful, her line one of the strongest among the order of light elves, and her magic was deadly. By all accounts, she was an outstanding archer, and she had a power over beasts, not to mention the entire Council and its subjects supporting her. Her actions were not simple precaution.

As capable as Junnie was, the tension apparent in her body spoke of the danger the changelings presented. Pitt was beyond powerful, and no one knew how many other fey might have been in play. She and her guard were prepared, because the risk was great.

They ran through the trees, heedless of the crunch of limbs

beneath their feet. The wolves muffled what sound they made, and if what Junnie had suspected was true, there would be no need for stealth. The changeling—or whatever the disturbance was—had clearly not managed to stay hidden. Thea dodged a thorn bush then ducked under a low-hanging vine, her boots finding ease in the path Junnie laid out for them. The forest was not as thick there, off of fey lands, and beneath the canopy, she caught glimpses of the lightening sky. She would feel better when the forest was lit around her, but even then, an unnatural warmth permeated her leather gear.

Junnie drew up short ahead of them, and the wolves came to a staggered stop with the rest of the guard. There was a whine from the animals as Junnie waited—whether listening or seeing through a creature's eyes, Thea couldn't know. The wolves danced their paws on the earth, impatient to go again. A breathless moment passed, and then Junnie was off, running full speed through the trees with the rest of the group at her back.

They broke into a clearing, where the rising sun spiked orange across the horizon. Junnie sped onto the field, coming to a stop with the draw of her bow. Behind her, Steed reached out as if to stop her but clearly unsure. Thea watched in horror as Junnie took aim not at the changeling fey in the center of a circle of charred earth and ash but at the figure in the sky—at the high fey lord.

"Stop!" Junnie commanded just as Veil took his own aim at the changeling below.

The fey lord's venomous gaze snapped to Junnie, and though the glare was not focused on Thea, she could feel the heat of it. It was not the heat of fire—it was not what had charred the earth. It was the heat of a summer sun, a warmth she could feel to her bones.

When Veil realized the head of the Council of light elves

had a weapon aimed at his chest, his expression shifted from anger to boiling rage. He seemed to consider leaving his intended target to come at Junnie, but there was something holding him there.

Thea's gaze tracked the scene and found a small, crumpled mass—Ruby.

Thea felt a sudden stab of fear, a sickness in the pit of her gut. She breathed, clasping and unclasping a fist while she decided if she could make it to Ruby's prone form and whether she could get past the battle or around it through the trees. Her other hand was slick with sweat, wrapped too tightly around the handle of her blade.

In front of Thea, Steed waited, watching Junnie with a wary eye.

"I demand you cease this now." Junnie's voice was no less than an order. It was not a threat that she might have shot at Veil. It was a warning that she had every intention of bringing him down.

"You dare," Veil hissed, shaking his head as his words fell off.

She more than dared. She'd warned him twice. Veil gestured toward the changeling standing beneath him, the being's gray skin a sickly hue. "This creature is *mine*. By law and by bargain."

By bargain. Thea looked again to the changeling, a fey so changed from when she'd seen him before. At the fates' dance ceremony on fey lands, he'd been vibrant and stunning, alluring, even as they'd known he was a horrid, horrid thing. He stood barefoot before them, apparently unconcerned, if one were to judge by his face. But the changelings could never be judged by appearance, because they could shift and deceive, hiding even pain. His color was off, though, his spiky white hair more like a strip of fur than it had seemed before. He did not look beautiful. She did not feel drawn to him in the way that made her skin crawl.

Pitt gripped a staff of ironwood, and though she thought it had once held a stone of blue, the gem atop it now glinted deep red. His robes were long, his fingers bare. Whatever other stones he possessed must have been nearer his person. Beyond him, in the low grass, something dark and small shifted closer. Thea's lips parted, and then she realized what she was seeing and purposely diverted her gaze. Steed stood in front of Thea, and she could see the strain in his posture, his need to act and inability to do so because of his duties as one of the Seven and the rulers between him and Ruby's prone form.

Thea glanced beside her, but everyone's eyes were on either the changeling or the fey lord. She dropped her cloak, laid down her sword, and willed herself to appear as small and nonthreatening as possible.

When she moved, she felt shifting behind her, but she did not look back. She was fast, and Steed had no time to prevent her from what she was about to do, not when he had his own task to deal with. He might have told another guard, but Thea had a fair mind of how Junnie operated, and she was confident that the head of Council would do nothing to stop her. She darted into the trees, feeling immediately that she'd crossed over that border and onto fey lands, not by the energy beneath the earth but by the lush and riotous growth. She felt a prickle of unease and knew, too, that she was being watched, that fey waited behind those leaves. She ran faster through the tangled forest, heedless of snapping branches or any sort of stealth. She heard shouted commands in the field, bits of the argument between lords.

She nearly screamed when she was lifted from the ground and again at the rush of being tossed, but the wind was knocked out of her when she thudded hard against the earth. She rolled out of the trees and into tall grass, gasping for air and wincing at the pain in her hip and shoulder. Had she not had the sense to draw in her limbs, she might have had bigger problems, but her hand found the dagger at her belt, and she grabbed it as she rolled into a crouch.

In the trees, a dark shadow shifted to and fro. She took in the tree line, the clearing, her new position. The fey had not been attacking her.

The fey had moved her nearer Ruby and the girl.

Thea dropped again to her stomach, mirroring the posture of the small raven-haired girl who'd been crawling through the grass toward Ruby. The girl had grown closer, having just reached the edge of that ring of cinder and ash, and she grabbed hold of Ruby's boot, dragging her body into the weeds. Thea scrambled toward them, helping to move Ruby to safer ground. Beyond them, threats and shouts still occupied the lords. There was a sudden, spine-chilling roar of a large cat, which sent Thea's hair to stand on end.

She glanced over her shoulder, and into the clearing leapt a dozen massive cats, black and golden with dotted fur. They sauntered closer to the changeling, circling him with a threat of their own.

The changeling smiled. "You cannot kill me," he said with an almost seductive purr. It was so out of place there, in the middle of her terror, and Thea realized the words had been spelled to life. They were low enough that she should not have heard, but she had a feeling that everyone within reach had.

There was a response to his words, and Thea felt her skin go cold, or maybe the entire clearing had lost a bit of its heat. She straightened slightly to find the source of it and saw the black leather and dark cloaks of her own uniform. A breath rushed out of her as she turned back to help the small girl heave Ruby away from what promised to be an unpleasant conflict.

The girl rolled Ruby onto her back, drawing her matted hair away from her face before unfastening the material at Ruby's neck. Ruby was bloodied but not badly. Thea wondered whether she'd been hit that hard or had merely used too much of her energy to fight the fey. She glanced up at the girl where they both leaned over Ruby and saw that the girl was streaked with blood and ash. "What happened?" Thea whispered.

"Potion." The girl didn't meet Thea's gaze, only kept working.

Thea could live with that. She leaned in, trying to scent what might have been used, and found the foul odor of spell-casting instead. She ran a hand over Ruby's cheek but could not feel any spells that had been placed on her. She closed her eyes, breathed in, and found a faint trace of yew and baneberry. It was strange that a changeling as powerful as this one would use a simple toxin to hit Ruby, but then Thea remembered the fates' dance.

She remembered he wanted Ruby alive.

Thea reached into the pouch at her waist, pulling free her meager supplies. She was missing several crucial ingredients, and she was fairly certain they were running out of time. She needed plants from within the fey forests, and she didn't have the time or ability to get them. The girl's fingers stilled where they were loosening Ruby's sword belt, and Thea listened for whatever had her spooked. She heard nothing, but when she raised her gaze, a cloud of high fey hovered around them.

The chill she expected over her skin did not come. It was warmth. It was Veil.

A bargain, he'd said. Thea stared at the ochre-skinned fey around her, their flesh painted with battle tattoos, waiting.

Veil had made a bargain with Ruby.

And there she was, likely to suffer permanent damage at the hands of that toxin if Thea didn't help her, if she couldn't get to the supplies she needed.

Plague it all, Thea was about to trust the task to a fey.

FREY

I STARED AT THE SCENE IN UTTER DISBELIEF. RUBY HAD bargained with a fey lord. They had made a trade. And Veil hovered, poised to end the changeling fey and release Ruby of her concerns in the matter, while Junnie held an arrow aimed for his chest.

Beside me, I felt Chevelle and the others taking in the scene, as well, making their own plans for action and possible response. The changeling had spoken his piece, declaring that none could destroy him without destroying fey lands.

I would not parley directly with that being, would not give him the satisfaction of a true audience. I let my gaze fall to Veil, first, out of respect for his part in Ruby's bargain only.

His wing flicked irritably. He glared at me. He needed not speak the words. He was bound by his trade with Ruby, and now my kin had him under threat.

I felt my mouth flatten into a thin line. Veil had reason enough to destroy Pitt after the betrayal during the fates' dance. We had stepped in to aid Veil, but that had gone farther than simply saving his skin. If Veil had failed, so had we. He still owed the changeling his due. My gaze found Junnie, but she did not take her eyes—or her aim—off Veil.

"What is this?" I asked her.

My cats prowled around the changeling, a pack of wolves watching the ordeal anxiously at Junnie's side. Steed stood just a step behind her, ready to act should I command him to do so.

"We must hold," Junnie answered. "There is more at work here than a simple bargain. The fate of a people, of *our* people, rests in that detestable being's plans."

"Your people," Veil roared.

I glared back at him.

The string of Junnie's bow held taut. I had seen her take a fey from the sky with it. I knew she could do so, even to one as powerful as Veil. Her arrow was tipped with iron and glistening with oil. She didn't intend to play their games. "Our people," Junnie echoed. She meant not just the light elves but all of them.

"And what of the fey?" I asked. My voice was quiet, even, but it seemed to echo through the clearing.

"They will be the cause of it all."

Veil hissed out a breath, and the clearing warmed to sweltering. Chevelle moved, but Veil stilled when he realized what I carried in my hand. The tip of the staff sat at my shoulder, its cool stone radiating energy that met his own. I could not be certain whether he hesitated out of caution or curiosity, but I couldn't spare it attention. I moved farther into the circle, angling myself between him above the changeling and Junnie, where she stood with her guard. "Have you considered that the fey lord might be more willing to parley without the use of your bow?" I asked.

"I have considered shooting him to save myself the breath," Junnie offered.

Somewhere behind me, Anvil covered a laugh.

I cleared my throat. "We are at peace with the fey. For the good of my people, I would prefer it stay so."

She drew a long breath and lowered her bow. No one missed the promise in her eyes for Veil. She would do it again should he give her the chance. I held my breath for one long moment, willing him *not* to break her trust. If he destroyed the changeling after being warned against it, he would have to answer to her. There would be nothing that would save him from that fate.

Junnie looked at me, and I saw the stress in her expression. "The changeling," she said. "He and the fey are responsible for the deadening of the base magic."

Veil was behind me in a flash, the wind of his speed brushing tendrils of my hair against my neck. He bent toward her, his tall, lean form casting a shadow over mine. "And now she dares to accuse us of creating the blight that threatens our own kind."

There was a sound behind us, and I turned, peering around Veil to find my guard and a few dozen fey warriors surrounding the changeling fey. He must have moved, shifted in some way that caused them alarm.

"Can we contain him until this matter is resolved?" I asked.

Veil ignored me, clearly having a single intention to kill the changeling.

"There is only one way," Junnie answered. The distaste in her voice said it was something dark, something the light elves would want no part of.

I blew out a breath, having no interest in spellcasting myself. "Then quickly, what should be done?"

Junnie did not trust Veil. She was right not to, and no one could argue that, but it made for poor negotiations. Her bright-and-blue eyes met mine. "The humans have a legend."

My skin went cold at the word, which had been echoing for a moon and could mean so much more.

"Isa has told me of their concerns, of the way their lands have turned and the cause of their migration these last seasons."

I felt Veil's heat subside, the presence of him shrinking at her words. So he'd heard them too. He'd known far more than he'd let on.

"If we've any chance to undo the damage, it will be with the changeling's help." Junnie let her gaze float to Veil. "And then you may kill him."

Veil's eyes narrowed, but he did not offer dispute.

"Then we bind him," I said. I turned to Chevelle, who'd been in earshot of our conversation. I supposed his estimation of Junnie had gone up, but that did little to ease my concern about using spells. The light elves had called our magic dark, but it was not the same sort of darkness used in castings. The power drawn was something else, something vile and nasty, and it had always made my skin crawl. Asher had used them often, but the spells could be unpredictable and could cause far more damage than anyone intended. To call them forth was a risk, and Chevelle was the only one present whom I trusted and who was also strong enough to cage the changeling fey. It made my stomach turn.

I didn't need to tell him to go ahead—he could read it on my face. He avoided looking at Veil, who hovered closely behind me, his wings curling just so about my side as Chevelle drew a pouch from his belt.

At the realization that he was about to be spelled, the changeling gripped his staff, ready to lift it then slam it to the ground. Veil shot a blast of power toward Pitt, barely skimming past Chevelle's arm. The changeling was struck, the staff knocked free of his hand, and I bit the inside of my cheek at the way Chevelle's shoulders went rigid and straight. I swung my own staff wide, nearly striking Veil with the tip, and he jerked back. I let him see the pledge of violent retaliation should he harm my Second in my gaze, but Veil only let his mouth crawl up into a lazy grin. "Swine," I muttered, turning my gaze to Steed.

He had been waiting, watching me, and at the jerk of my chin, he went around the guards and beasts surrounding Pitt to assist Thea with Ruby. The changeling hadn't hurt her badly, we'd been told, but that didn't mean I would trust the word of a fey. I wanted one of my Seven with her.

We moved closer, and some of Junnie's guard relieved the others of their charge. Pitt might have looked frail, but he was one of the most powerful fey alive. I wasn't certain how long he'd gone without crossing the fey borders to restore his energy, but he'd surely taken ample stones when he'd left. He would not be easy to hold, even though Junnie had likely ordered her men to restrain him from all sides as soon as they'd arrived. Even though he'd battled Ruby and Veil and countless other fey, he remained deadly.

"Your new guard?" I asked Veil, gesturing toward a line of ocher-skinned warriors with the top of my head. They'd decorated themselves with battle tattoos, curving lines and symbols that counted their dead. Several were nearly covered in the designs.

His expression went flat.

"Decided if you could not trust your own men you would find the most untrustworthy lot you could?"

He rolled his gaze skyward. "They are not the *most* untrustworthy."

"Hmm." I supposed he was right. It was, after all, likely the changelings who deserved that title.

We settled into silence as Chevelle cast powder over the

ashen ground around Pitt. The changeling's body was still flat after Veil's strike, and Junnie's men held him in place. Pitt was reserving his magic, it seemed, holding back words that would require energy to spell into life.

Grey and Anvil stood and drew their swords, ready to move wherever they were needed, with Rhys and Rider farther back toward the trees. I knew it was torture for Grey not to be able to go to Ruby, but it was not the worst he had suffered. What had happened the last time was fresh in our minds, and we would hold to our duties first, so that we might walk away with everyone intact—not sacrifice the whole for one. It was why I'd let him come.

The changeling's staff lay on the burnt earth out of his reach, but that didn't mean he was safe. None of this was safe, none of it certain. Pitt was more than clever, and he was known to have several plans in place, a tangled web of options ready if he needed them.

I watched as Chevelle's arms moved with steady grace, the motions and words drawing power from the earth. It was not simply unpleasant—it made me want to turn and run. A foul smell came with the darkness, and smoke rolled into something viscous before shifting back to smoke again. It was not some simple charm. It was stronger, more potent and dangerous enough to be able to hold the changeling in bonds.

Chevelle would bind him from reaching his magic, the way Council and Asher had done to me so long ago. He would be spared his memories, but that was all. The bonds were a slippery thing, as I had proven, and there was no guarantee that some part of his magic couldn't get through. Chevelle would follow the binding with other spells meant to physically restrain Pitt. We had no other way to cage him, not when the smallest misstep could give him his break, not when it took a fey lord and a dozen men to hold him.

Veil was right that killing him would have been easier. We might as well have been attempting to pin a wild animal with our bare hands.

Beyond Chevelle and the others, my cats prowled the deep grass. There was a shifting near Ruby, the movements of Steed, Thea, and the girl, Willa. I could see the top of Willa's head, and then Ruby rose to her feet. Thea tried to restrain Ruby, and Steed steadied her by the other arm. Willa's sword came up, and my mouth dropped open, ready to call an alert, but Steed let go of Ruby to grab the girl's arm, and as Thea ducked away from a wild swing, Ruby darted toward the clearing, toward the changeling fey.

Veil cleared his throat, and suddenly I realized he held my arm. Before I could get a word out, I understood.

He was helping Ruby. They had made a bargain.

I didn't know whether it was a warning or he would strike me down if I meant to stop her. At my incredulity, his mouth turned down. He clearly did not want to have his hand forced in the matter.

The tip of Junnie's arrow slid carefully past my face, aimed again at the fey lord's chest.

Veil glared down at Junnie. "Would you *kindly* stop doing that?"

It was not begging, not from a fey, but I faltered at his phrasing.

Junnie had no such compunction. "Give me one good reason why I should."

"The halfling knows what she's doing," he said flatly.

Junnie and I looked back to the field, where Ruby was spinning deftly past Council soldiers and warrior fey, whip in hand. The changeling moved just as she neared him, and she struck out, wrapping the barbed leather around his chest. It constricted his arms and burned him, but through it all, Chevelle never missed a beat. Ruby tore open the changeling's cloak, the material above her weapon ripping to shreds. Around his neck hung a long chain, woven with spelled twine, no doubt, and spelled to stay on his person. She jerked it free, screaming as it burned into her flesh.

Anvil and Grey had moved for her, and she lobbed the stone toward them before collapsing. Grey caught Ruby just before she hit the earth, tossing her easily over his shoulder to haul her away as Anvil guarded his back. Rhys and Rider shifted their positions to either side of Chevelle as the smoke rose higher and the spell wove tighter around the changeling, Pitt. His color had turned a dull greenish gray, something earthen and sickly at once.

I resisted the urge to distance myself, to step back and away from the smoke, from Pitt, from all of it. Junnie stood at my other side, having clearly come to understand that Veil only meant to prevent me from restraining Ruby before she retrieved the jewel.

We stood together, three kingdoms' lords who had nearly watched it all fall apart at the hands of a single changeling fey.

FREY

THE SMOKE SETTLED AROUND CHEVELLE, CURLING INTO THIN wisps before falling to the ground like ash. The stench of sulfur and sourness lingered, but that was all. The casting was done. Pitt lay stunned in the center of the circle of charred earth and soldiers, and I wondered briefly what Ruby had endured before we arrived. A spike of irritation flashed through me, because it was not what she'd been through but what she had *done*—what she and Veil had done.

I brushed past him, ignoring the flip of his wing. Grey was settling Ruby's body, limp and smeared with ash, down onto unburnt grass. Her eyes flitted open, and what I saw in them made me ill. I might have taken it as an apology, but I knew Ruby. She'd have done it all again if given the chance. Grey looked up at me with a pained expression, and I lay a hand on his shoulder. Thea stood back as if waiting for permission to approach, and I had the strange sense that the girl who had reacted without thought so often was doing that out of deference to me.

My head hurt. I needed to get away from the indistinct

buzz of so many human minds in the distance to get some peace. I started to gesture Thea closer, but Junnie was there, leaning over Ruby to assess her wounds. I knew Junnie would take care of her.

I turned, finding Chevelle as he cleaned his hands from the spellwork on a strip of dark cloth. I walked closer, scenting the oil that coated the rag. Chevelle might have acted as if he'd no issue with spellcasting, but that didn't stop him from taking every precaution to wipe the evidence of it clean. He did not look up at me, but I didn't need him to. Just being near him was enough.

Steed approached, holding the girl Willa tightly by the shoulder. He thrust her toward Chevelle. "Is this one yours?"

Chevelle frowned at the girl, whose eyes were defiant. It was not the girl's fault, really. Ruby had given her orders. And if Ruby and Veil knew the stone was so important, she might have actually saved them from some unpleasant fate. Chevelle's stare seemed to be enough to crumble her silence.

"It was clearly not my intention to actually strike down the healer," Willa said. "I only had to provide my lead time to escape."

Chevelle shoved the oiled cloth into the pouch at his hip then brushed his palms together and let a free hand rest on the hilt of his sword.

The girl paled. Ruby might have been one of the Seven, but Chevelle was Second, the head of the guard.

He let her sweat for another long moment then gestured for one of the guards to take custody of her. I felt a little bad for her—it was going to be a terribly long ride home.

When she was gone, Steed and I shared a glance that said he had more to discuss. My grip tightened around the staff, and I wondered what else we had missed. I would not forgive Veil for the distractions at the castle or for him delaying us at the border, but I was ready to go. "It's time to take leave," I said. "Steed, if you can assist us with a fresh set of mounts"—I glanced at Ruby behind us, with Junnie and Grey at her sides—"we'll leave who we can to wait with Ruby."

Chevelle nodded, his gaze meeting Anvil's across the clearing. Anvil held the stone Ruby had risked much for as she'd ripped it off the changeling's neck. "Cursed fairies," I muttered, brushing a hand over my face.

"Cursed fairies," Chevelle echoed. His gaze was on mine, but I could feel the heat of Veil behind me.

"I'll take the changeling." Veil's voice was level, and it was not a question.

I sighed and turned to face him. "You know Junnie will not accept that."

"It's not her decision to make," he said. His arms were crossed over his chest, all pretense and posturing gone. The extended energy required to hold Pitt there instead of just ending him had weighed even on Veil.

There was a hiss in the clearing behind us, and I knew Veil had only professed his intent to get us to turn around. The fey were trying to steal the changeling as we faced the other direction.

I could hear the smirk in Chevelle's voice. "It may be difficult, given that he's spelled against fey magic."

Veil's face twisted into a sort of snarl. I tipped the end of my staff ever so slightly, daring him to move forward. He took note.

I very much liked my new weapon, even if I'd yet to test it on fey grounds.

"We will conference on the matter," Junnie said from beside us. She'd left Ruby—and likely instructions for how best to care for her—with Thea and Grey. "For now, the changeling will be held at the encampment, where an appropriate holding cell has already been established." Veil and I both gave her speculative glances over that, but she went on. "I suggest that a representative from each of your lands stay as witness to what we are able to draw from him."

She did not have to say why. Veil would not travel so far from the base magic, and I could not bear to stay near so many humans. No one could trust that leaving the changeling with Veil would end in anything but murder, and I certainly didn't want to drag him back to our own lands. It was the closest, most acceptable venue and the fastest way to get information from him. "Once we find the source and cure for the blight, we will meet on neutral ground."

So it was not something she thought would be an easy fix, but that was unsurprising, I supposed, given that Veil had been willing to bargain with me to get some sort of reprieve from the human encroachment.

Veil glared down at Junnie, his distaste for her seeming to grow by the minute. He looked to me, apparently deciding I was the authority or just through with the woman who persisted in trying to kill him. "Any land that is not fey is not neutral, and you know it," he said.

"Fine," I replied, knowing he was right. Without access to the base magic, Veil could not be on equal ground. And as it was, his ground was growing smaller every day. "What do you propose, then, the border? I'm certain that will be private enough for your liking."

His wing twitched. He closed his eyes. "Fine. I open my house to you, upon my invitation and under guarantee of my sworn protection…" He gestured vaguely through the air as he muttered, indicating the myriad of promises to be made by a fey lord.

I glanced at Junnie, who seemed satisfied by the oath.

Surely, she could see I needed to get out of there. "Who do you want?" I asked.

"Anvil will suffice," she said.

I nodded. "Anvil and a dozen guard, then. Grey and Steed will bring Ruby as soon as she's well."

"It will not be long," Junnie answered. I felt the tension ease from my shoulders, as she'd not meant merely Ruby's recovery but also her discovery of what secrets the changeling held. "Let us meet in two days' time."

Veil flicked some gesture at his own men, and fey descended from sky and canopy, rustling the leaves and blowing away ash. The clearing was suddenly washed free of the scent of spellcasting, instead smelling of summer winds and flowering vines. There were twenty of them, tall and ocher-skinned, with black dotted wings—warriors left with Junnie to represent the kingdom of fey.

The humans were going to be terrified.

THEA

THEA SAT WITH RUBY FOR THE REST OF THAT DAY AND throughout the night. It was well past dawn, and Ruby's fevers and weakness had subsided. Junnie had tended the other wounds as well, sending Thea with instructions for further care and suggestions on how she might force Ruby into actually allowing her ministrations.

It would be easy enough, Thea thought, given that everyone knew that the following day, there would be a call for a meeting with the fey lord. If what they'd said was true, they were all fortunate that the changeling wanted Ruby alive. Otherwise, his plans would have played out with no one the wiser. The fey lands would slowly have been starved for power, and the fey, needing that energy to sustain themselves, would have spread into the surrounding kingdoms in search of a way to live again. Nothing good could come of a desperate, dying race of beings set on stealing energy, but only worse could come from the fey.

Thea stood alone with the horses while the others prepared supplies, watching Ruby where she sat leaning against a tree, stitching her uniform back into order. Both kept their backs to the humans, who were bustling about the encampment since daylight had come. There was something quietly unsettling about the beings, and no one except maybe the fey relished being near them.

Thea shook off a chill as she recalled the predatory glances Veil's men had given the humans. She'd not spent much time around fey, all in all, but the more she did, the less she wanted of it.

Ruby and Thea did not speak. After Ruby's health had proven to be good enough, the stress of finding her and making her safe had gone, to be replaced with a new sort of weight, one that was less urgent and more like the dangers the kingdoms had faced in the past. Thea tried not to think of how many had been lost in the massacre so long ago, because what was done was done, and there was no good that would come by keeping it near. She would not forget—none of them would—but remembering and dwelling were two separate spheres. Everyone had lost something from the tragedy of the massacre, and most, like Barris, had lost far more than she had.

She vowed anew to work hard, to do what she could to help her father, and to keep her focus on doing right by the guard.

A hand slid slowly behind Thea's as she brushed a palm across the shoulder of her horse, shadowing her movements with slow, easy grace.

"He's one of my favorites," Thea said. She was glad the animal had survived their ride through fey lands, and she hoped it would remain so during their return. Behind her, Steed did not reply, but she felt him there, his steady breath and even pulse a signal to the animals that they were safe and that all was well.

He moved to lift a pack onto the horse, and Thea backed one step away.

Ruby did not look up from her sewing. "When we return, Steed should take you farther into the stables, where he keeps the absolute best of the stock." Even with her face turned down, Thea could see the small twitch at the edge of Ruby's lips as she added, "Why, even Lord Freya's beast is there."

Steed froze in his fastenings, giving his sister a look that spoke of utter betrayal.

Thea bit back her own grin at his response. She'd lived in Camber and had been on the castle grounds long enough to have heard some of the better gossip. It shouldn't have surprised them both that she already knew that Frey had named the horse she'd been given after Steed.

She shrugged one shoulder. "Not as if I've not named animals after him before."

Steed turned his wary gaze to her, and Ruby cracked a grin, waiting for the payoff. Thea's tone was steady. "There was a wiry boar we had for years. The cursed thing was so stubborn we could never get him to root anywhere inside of a pen. He would dig out, chase Cora around the yard, and then burrow beneath the porch. We finally had to eat him."

Steed's expression was flat.

Ruby snorted.

Grey approached the group, his attention solely for Ruby and her easy mood. Thea could remember that when they were younger, he would always greet her with a comment about her causing trouble. He did not do so that day. "We leave now. Anvil and the rest will depart after dawn to meet with the fey lord. We should return to the castle before Frey and the others have gone."

Ruby had said they'd all been delaying action until after sunrise just to annoy Veil, but Thea wasn't certain what that meant. Ruby didn't seem to mind waiting longer, though, as Grey stared down at her and she went about repairing the leather of her garment.

He tucked a thumb into his knife belt. "Would you like me to haul you from the ground?"

She glanced up with a look that dared him to.

He smirked. "I have orders that supersede yours, I'm afraid."

Ruby's face paled. Thea supposed that was the reprimand she knew would be coming from the Lord of the North. Ruby slipped the needle back into her pouch, jerking the leather bits into place as she stood. Considering what she'd been through, she didn't look half bad, but she kept fiddling with the straps and belts, working to get them into proper order.

Grey stood very near, watching, but he didn't touch her.

Thea remembered that, too—the way he'd always been there and the way Ruby had never allowed him in. It was because of her mother and what had happened. Thea's gaze trailed away from the exchange and found Steed watching her.

They'd both been younger when Ruby came along, and it was easy to forget what life had been like before. The fey came of age so fast, and even if she was only half fey, Ruby had seemed to catch up with them all in the blink of an eye. It was as if she'd always been there.

Thea supposed that for Steed, the feeling was even stronger. She shook herself from the ruminations and took over the task of readying her horse. Steed had told her not to let the task go to anyone else's hand when she'd the choice, but she'd stood by and let him do it for her. She didn't suspect he counted as anyone else, though.

They mounted up, and as they rode past the makeshift houses of the humans there, the Council guard did not pay them mind. Junnie did not come out to see them off, either—

she would not leave the changeling alone, especially not with a horde of high fey killers on hand. Isa did come to bid them farewell, though. She stood petite and proud among a line of Council guard, the only one of the group who met their eyes. She inclined her head at Thea then murmured something soft to Ruby and to Steed.

It might have been easy to presume that the girl felt alone there, but she was far from that. She had the guard and her gardens, and she tended to uncountable humans. The girl would likely never have felt at home at Junnie's side while she was head of Council, and being a halfling probably weighed heavily on her beneath the watchful eye of so many light elves.

Isa was not made for growing and working earth. Her father had been a powerful dark elf, and he'd given her a bit of that magic, surely, in addition to whatever let her into the minds of the humans.

Thea pursed her lips, and Steed drew his horse up beside hers. "What's wrong?"

She shook her head. "Nothing. I just…" She glanced behind them, past her own guard, who was all dressed in black, to the bright hair and light robes of the Council sentries—to the humans.

Steed waited.

She sighed. "It doesn't—I mean, you know how the breeding works." His face pinched on one side, clearly trying to puzzle what she was angling at. "It doesn't make sense, is all. You'd have to have at least old blood"—she frowned—"at least *any* of a bloodline to pass a trait like that on."

Steed's expression fell into something reserved.

Thea bit her cursed tongue. She was a guard. She had no business talking about a Council head's charge who also happened to be blood of the dark elf lord whom Thea herself had volunteered under.

But that was the thing that was bothering her. Isa was only related to Frey through Asher. She should only have been able to access that dark magic. Frey's power, and her ability to reach the mind of animals, came from her mother's line—from Junnie's line.

Frey's mother was Eliza. Eliza's mother, Junnie's sister, was Vita, the light elf who was rumored to have been stolen by Asher. Thea had heard countless versions of the tale: how he'd spirited her away in the night and how she'd gone willingly, having longed for a being as powerful as she was. Sometimes, they were told as romantic tales, sometimes cautionary. But in the end, Vita had always died. Grief had taken her, and no one dared to tell fancy tales or spin legends from them.

The sisters Vita and Junnie were a pair of the most powerful light elves from one of the most powerful lines. No one was surprised to find the whispers of a special talent among them to be true. But when Asher had taken her, when a light elf had sat upon the seat at a dark elf's side, brazen upon a throne, it had caused a shift within the kingdoms. Thea had heard the stories, though her father had never spoken of them himself. By the time Eliza was born, the rift in the union of the kingdoms of all elves had grown into a chasm, filled with dissent and distrust.

And then Eliza had borne the child of a human: a halfbreed.

And the old Order of Light Elves had turned on the kingdom of the dark. The coup had taken hold, and the events leading to the massacre had fallen into motion. The Council had killed untold numbers. So many had been lost, light and dark alike, and every human who had been called to battle, every human Eliza had thrust into that world as her last-ditch effort to save her daughter, to end the reign of her father, had been slaughtered in their makeshift army. They were like chattel.

As they made their way farther from the settlement, Steed stayed silent at Thea's side. It was not until they'd passed through the trees and into the next clearing, the one that brought them to the edge of the fey forest, that he answered her confusion. "The girl does not possess that same talent," he said.

Thea's eyes snapped to him, but Steed kept his posture straight, his gaze on the forest.

"She can only reach the humans."

Thea stared, bewildered. But he was right. The girl had never once seemed to attempt using the power on a beast, not even that giant dog. And the wolves had seemed to terrify her. "So how can she reach humans when she can't touch a simple beast?"

Steed inclined his head, because yes, *that* was the question.

FREY

I waited at the window of Anvil's study, dressed and ready for battle with the fey. Veil had promised us protection, but that did not mean any of us would come unprepared for a fight. We should have gone already, but I had something pressing to take care of first.

Kieran opened the door, leading in my guests.

I turned to find Thea, laden with a half-dozen satchels, followed by Ruby, Grey, and Steed. Thea looked up, searching for a place to settle her burden, and went still at the sight of me. She opened her mouth, possibly to apologize, then snapped it shut again. She made to leave, but Kieran stood in her way.

"Thea," I said, bringing her attention back to me.

"Lord Freya." She managed a sort of incline to her head, more than I expected, given that the rest of her was loaded with what were likely Ruby's bags.

I could think of no other reason why she would be required to carry them herself. Ruby would not have wanted anything she planned to use for tonics handled by someone who didn't understand the proper method of dealing with them.

With my arms crossed behind my back, I straightened to face her. I inclined my own head, and for a moment, Thea looked as if she might step back. "Thank you," I explained, "for your continued service to my guard."

She seemed confused, as if she hadn't realized she'd not only kept Steed alive when he was attacked by the fey the last time but had also risked her neck to stay with him when he'd traveled to find Junnie and then into fey lands. And more recently, again, knowing what was at stake, she'd stayed at his side and risked her own self in order to aid him and to aid Ruby.

"You have consistently offered support to my Seven and have gone above and beyond in your duties. It will not be forgotten."

Thea went pale. She glanced around the room as if searching for someone to help her, but no one did.

"You may go." I glanced at Kieran, who nodded, seemingly understanding that she'd seemed a bit overwhelmed. He followed her out, and I knew that he would give her a copy of the missive I'd drawn up to send her parents.

Once the door closed behind them, Steed and Grey stood formally at either side of Ruby. She had her head down, but after a moment, she drew a long breath and faced me with an emotion that seemed to be made of more mourning than regret. She stepped forward, reaching out to hand me the signet from her uniform, a small carved medallion showing the symbols of my crest, the badge of the Seven.

I stared at her. "You dare attempt to abandon your duties after what you have done?"

My tone was sharp, and Ruby flinched, but she didn't draw back her hand.

"Is that what you think? That after all this, you can just walk away?"

I took a step toward her, forcing her outstretched hand to become an awkward gesture, her offering uncomfortable in every sense. "You have risked the lives of your Seven and of our guard—of every single person in this kingdom. Everyone who relies on me, on *us* to keep their skin."

Her expression fell, but I only moved closer.

"You think that by protecting us from a changeling, you're making a sacrifice that has to be made. That decision is not up to you. You are of the Seven. You do not get to choose us over you." I took one more step, pressing her further. "This is not your sacrifice to make, Summit."

Ruby stared up at me, her green eyes glistening with fear.

I didn't know whether it was fear that I was angry at her, that she was about to lose everything she'd meant to save, or that I would actually let her go. My voice was low and level when I said, "Put that badge on, now. I do not want to see you without it again."

Her fingers curled around the metal as she bore it before her chest.

I held her gaze. "For what you have done, you owe the Seven and this kingdom your service." It sounded like a sentence, but I didn't care. Ruby had to understand.

She swallowed hard.

Suddenly, I could not look at her or let her speak. "Take her to her rooms," I ordered Grey. "She'll submit to Junnie's instructions for her care and stay on castle grounds until our return."

Grey gave a slight nod and took Ruby by the elbow. His hand was still marked with evidence of nearly being burned alive.

"Oh, and Grey?" I said to his back. "If a single fey sets foot or wing anywhere near her, I expect them to be shot from the sky."

He glanced back at me over his shoulder, and I had no doubt that he would happily comply.

When the door closed behind them, I let my shoulders ease and my gaze fall to Steed. "I'm nearly afraid to ask, but what have you learned that merits time before we leave for this congress?"

~

BY THE TIME we reached Veil's home, it was late in the day. He had met us at the border, despite the fact that Junnie was transporting a bound changeling through fey lands. I supposed I shouldn't have been surprised that he'd allowed her to go without escort, given that he'd made it clear that he wanted Pitt dead—and whether or not Junnie was taken with him in an attempt, the fey lord likely did not care.

When we approached the tall trees that served as support for his abode, Veil glanced at me with a bit of a smirk. I frowned up at the structure, all open air and glass, remembering how I'd been lifted to enter the last time. Veil's heliotropes were gone, and I suspected Chevelle would not allow the high fey lord to hoist him from the ground, not that I'd even trust him to do it.

"We don't have time for games," I said.

Veil barked a mirthless laugh and launched into the air.

From behind us, several of his new fey allies moved in to offer us aid.

Chevelle did not need to give me a look to indicate he was displeased. He did it anyway. I sighed, holding my staff carefully away from the fey as he took hold of the weapons belt across my back and shoulder. I glanced at Anvil, where he stood with his arms crossed over his wide chest, and he said, "I'll wait here."

I threw him a grin until the fey whisked Chevelle and me off the ground. Rhys and Rider waited farther back, in the thick of the trees, and a few dozen of the guard were scattered between. I felt the minds of some of Junnie's wolves nearby but little else in the shadows beyond.

The fey deposited us onto the glass floor of Veil's home, its surface like crystal, heated into being long ago by the fire of a powerful fey. I had a sudden, sickening flash of a memory of the last time I was there, and then the urge to snap my staff onto the glass and let it all fall to the forest floor shook me.

"Lord Freya," Veil purred as if he'd read my thoughts.

I gritted my teeth and took a breath. *This is not before. I am no longer trapped between bad and worse.*

Veil was the one in that position, and I only needed to do what I could to stop the spread of the deadened energy, preferably in a way that didn't involve slaughtering an entire population of beings.

He watched me but not in the way the others had so many times before when I was bound and they feared I might crack at any moment. I met his gaze.

"Juniper awaits." Veil gestured toward the tall amber windows that separated the space. The glass was a haze of color, providing at least some semblance of privacy between rooms, but the rest was made of open, windowed walls that stared out over the canopy of trees. Veil's kingdom stretched as far as the eye could see.

Chevelle's arm brushed mine, a reminder to stay focused. I had him, and I had the staff, but a bout of temper could do more than a little damage. I straightened, securing my grip on my staff as we followed Veil into the next room.

Junnie stood near the far wall, decidedly avoiding the view

and its staggering drop. Beside her waited several of her new Council guard, resplendent in their formal uniforms. Kneeling on the floor before her was the changeling, Pitt, his arms bound behind his back and a metal lash securing his head to stay bowed. I resisted the urge to glance at Chevelle. He'd bound the changeling with spells, and Pitt wouldn't be able to shift forms. It seemed a cruel device, and I had to remind myself that the changeling had tried to end not just a handful of us but apparently also a kingdom of fey.

Veil's warriors lined the other walls, and at some unseen command, they exited the room. He sauntered to a small table laden with crystal goblets and decanters to pour himself a glass of wine. The fey lord turned, lifting the bottle in invitation, but I only looked at him. No one would accept a fey offering of food or drink. It didn't factor that if he'd wanted to poison us, it was only a matter of brushing a toxin on our skin —it was the principle of it.

Junnie and four of her guard were the only ones present outside of Chevelle, Veil, Pitt, and me, and I turned to her. "Let's have it."

Junnie nodded. "The changeling is guilty of high crimes. The fey lord can have him back."

Veil swirled the wine in his glass, his mouth a steady line.

"We have been able to extract no vital information from him directly," she said, "but the humans have provided evidence of intrusion by his kind."

"Intrusion," I repeated.

"They have been journeying into human territory for an unknown amount of time, stealing children, terrorizing entire populations into scattering and resettling again and again."

Veil's swirling stilled.

Junnie took a long breath. "The changelings have been herding them toward fey lands for a generation or more."

The room went silent before the swell of heat warmed my bones. There was a strange sort of tingling in my palm, where I tightly gripped the ironwood staff.

"There is no direct indication that Pitt was solely at fault, but no other changeling holds sway over so many of his kind, and we are confident that none could keep it secret for this long otherwise." She tapped a long finger on the woven belt at her hip. "He was the only one with a contingency plan in place. If nothing else, he was aware of the deceit and put the fey lands at risk, as well as our own." She glanced at Veil. "I no longer have use for him."

At her words, Veil moved, by all appearances ready to unleash a righteous fury, but before he'd crossed the space, a sharp *crack* snapped through the building. I stepped back automatically, bracing my footing, but nothing was there.

The floor had fallen away from my feet. I was plummeting with shattered bits of glass as the entirety of the floor exploded into fragments and dust, and then I was jerked to a stop as Veil grabbed the straps crossing my back. Something brushed my leg, but I was swung away from it as Veil moved. Junnie dangled from a tree limb at some distance, with two of her men farther down. Heart racing, I searched for Chevelle, but Veil still had hold of me, and we were diving toward the ground. We burst through leaves and limbs, splinters of broken wood spraying my skin.

He slammed to a stop a short distance from the ground, tossing me to land on my feet as he spun to find Pitt. I scrambled forward to find my staff, too harried to be sick at the thought of whatever might have happened to Chevelle or Junnie. I huffed and turned again but could see nothing but the destruction of glass and trees. A snap of power blasted into me, knocking me off my feet and clearing away the bulk of the debris. Trees crashed into their brethren, heedless of what elf or fey stood in their way. I could see figures moving in the distance, Anvil and the sentries and what appeared to be wolves, which meant Junnie was alive.

I shot a glare at the nearest of Veil's men. "Get Juniper Fountain safely to the ground."

He obeyed without hesitation, and I turned again, searching for Chevelle. The scent of wildfire and spice filled the forest, amber glass and amber skin flashing with the late-day sun. I looked up, horrified to see open sky. Nothing was left of the structure but bits of frame and limbs. Winged creatures circled overhead but none that I could use. They were fey, not animals, and I could see no more than with my own eyes.

I screamed, "Chevelle," but he did not respond. Veil was gone, chasing after the changeling, and his fey were plucking Junnie and her men from the trees above. I cursed violently and crudely, and a light, tinkling snigger rang through the trees.

I spun, furious, and found the sweet face of a changeling fey, smiling as she held my ironwood staff gingerly between two fingers.

"Liana," I hissed.

She only shrugged.

"Where is Chevelle?"

"Snared, I'm afraid. Taken in your stead, as it seems the fey lord took you safely in hand before they could do so themselves."

My insides turned to ice, my voice a whisper. "Who is *they*?"

She frowned. "Why, Pitt's men, of course." She handed me the staff as if she were eager to be rid of it, and when I touched the wood, I could feel that the cold had come from its stone. Liana said, "Tell me you didn't think he would leave his capture unanswered."

"He's bound."

Liana sighed, the sound spelled out of her with a wisp of frosty air. "Only by his body and magic. No one tied the hands of his network."

"Where is my Second?" My words cut through the forest, and Liana's pretense of an easy mood fell away.

"They'll take him to Hollow Forest. The changeling will want him alive."

THEA

Thea stood in the narrow corridor of the upper levels of the castle, working to still her trembling hands as she read a missive from the Lord of the North. She had barely managed the standing, the stilling, or the reading when she understood. "This cannot be real," she had whispered, afraid to even speak aloud. But it had been true and done before she'd even held it in her hand. The parchment she'd been given, which still rested in her pocket, had been merely a copy, Kieran had said. The first had been sent to Camber, where it would have been delivered to her mother and her father.

It would tell them of the great deeds she had done, protecting the kingdom, serving with honor, and aiding the Lord.

Thea sighed again, running a hand over the horse at her side. The trembling had settled, the shock of it gone. Nothing was left but relief. It hadn't stopped her from needing fresh air and time to herself.

What the Lord of the North had done for Thea and for her family would ease every burden they would ever face. They'd been given favor, certainly, but the included reward had given them reprieve. Her father would be able to cease his worry, and her mother could spend less time tending to her work and more time helping him heal. It was enough, and if they decided to do so, they might even share their good fortune with her sister.

It was enough that they needed never to worry about their survival again.

THEA FELT Steed's presence in the stable long before she realized she'd become aware of it. When she did, she let him watch her and decide whether or not he would approach. It wasn't that he was a wild thing or that she thought he might balk. It was that she did not need to rush him.

He did come to her, slowly and quietly with his steady gait. She closed her eyes as he fell to a stop behind her, so close that it hurt. He reached to place his hand behind hers and they moved. He ran a palm over the shoulder of the mare in tandem with Thea's, not touching her but moving with her.

Thea's hair was in a complicated braid piled at the crown of her head, compliments of Ruby, and the cool air brushed her heated skin. Steed leaned down, pressing his lips to the spot below her jaw, where her pulse pounded in a steady beat. She raised her hand to touch him, to hold him there against her, and his face turned to press another kiss onto the delicate skin inside her wrist. She sighed, leaning into him, letting the feel of him settle her further. He was greatly preferable to a mare for that.

"There are options better suited," Steed said quietly, "and men who would not allow you to be dragged into such troubles." Thea's eyes snapped open, her mouth flattening into a thin line. She withdrew from his embrace, turning to glower at him, at the man who… *What? Intended to be strong and… whatever he thought it was to sacrifice himself for my sake?*

She was having none of it.

"Have you any idea how absolutely insulting that is?"

He stared at her, clearly not having any idea.

His mouth parted to speak, but she went on. "I make my own decisions, and aside from my duties as a guard, I'll not be told what should be done."

He moved to shake his head, to argue that was not his intention.

She crossed her arms. "For you to say to me that you do not want me... that I am not well-suited enough…"

The color drained from his face, and Thea knew she had him. Whatever noble gesture he'd intended was gone. She'd trapped him between being a brute and forcing her to accept his advice to seek someone—*what, milder?* She didn't know. Maybe he would explain that she wasn't what he wanted.

Thea knew that was a lie. He did want her. He only understood that being with him was not the smartest, safest choice for her.

She didn't care.

There was a sound in the distance, somewhere over the pasture wall. Their eyes went to it, both of them on alert. Thea had not meant to leave her argument hanging like that, but the cry in the distance had sounded bad. She drew her knife and followed Steed across the grass toward the gate.

They were through the gate before the cry sounded again, and then they were running full pelt.

Light flashed across the sky, scenting the air with the electric charge of a storm. A tingle raced over Thea's skin, and then a too-warm wind brought the scent of amaranth and violets. She cursed, shoving her blade into its sheath and darting away from Steed to duck into a watch station. She grabbed a bow, nearly knocking into another guard, and then was back, running through the passages and archways toward the main gate. There was a burst of shouting, a mass of guards falling into rank, and then the shush-shush of their arrows cutting through the sky. Thea stopped, searching the crowd, and a solid thump sounded beside her as a fey fell to the ground.

She stared for an instant at the steel-tipped shaft jutting brokenly from the fey man's side, and then was knocked back as someone rushing past brushed into her. She shook herself, running not toward the gate but back inside the castle walls. Thea was no true warrior, and she could not be of immediate help, but if the fey were coming for battle, she needed to get her supplies. She sprinted through the corridors toward Ruby's rooms. They had left the supplies there, all of them waiting to be sorted and stored, to be prepped for tonics and medicines.

When she turned the corner of Ruby's hall, she found Steed, white-faced and still. Her chase fell to a stop in front of him, her chest heaving in a breath.

Steed's eyes left the open doorway of Ruby's room, a trickle of blood running from the crown of his head and over his cheek. "They're gone," he whispered, his voice low and rasping. "Both of them."

And then he fell, crashing into Thea and shoving them both against a wall. She shouted out, but more guards were already coming, and they grabbed Steed's limp form to settle him onto the ground.

She smelled it right away. "Poison!" Thea shouted, covering her face with an arm. "Get back, all of you!"

The guards dragged Steed down the corridor, his leather boots scuffing limply against the stone. She cursed, kicked the wall, and cursed again because of the pain. The antidote she needed was inside. Thea tore the fabric of her sleeve, tied a strip of it around her face to cover her mouth and nose, and then, wincing at the light through watery eyes, ran into the space that had been blasted with toxin by the fey.

Ruby's rooms were a disaster of overturned furniture and burned fabric, her floor littered with the bodies of fey. Thea stepped over one, his wide brow covered in thorned tattoos. She hurried toward the broken table, stumbled, knocked into the wall, and then righted herself to grab blindly at the mixes covering the floor. She prayed she'd gathered the right ones and that her supply had not been tainted with something worse then ran back for the door.

She got two steps through it before she crashed to the ground. She gasped, sucking air through the thick cloth covering her face, and a pair of sentries dragged her farther down the hall. She shoved her hand at them, the leaves and powder sticking to her palm. The face above her only stared, but the hand of another reached across him to take the offering while she coughed and pressed her cheek to the cool stone floor. Her knees ached from where she'd crashed into it before, and she could feel the wetness of blood.

She lost a few moments to darkness then felt the rag jerked from her face. The sharp scents of plateroot and marigold burned her nose. She coughed again, pushing herself up so that she might smack whoever was shoving it into her face. She reached out blindly and took hold of the root, breaking a piece in half to chew. It was horrid. She gagged, her eyes and mouth watering, and waved the broken half toward the sentries. "Steed." She managed the single hoarse word before she gagged again.

There was a rustling sound, shouting, and rushing footfalls in the distance as Thea tried to blink away the tears. Someone handled her a flagon of water. She splashed it over her face. When her gaze cleared, she took a swig to wash down the vile taste, and said, "Ruby. They've got Ruby and Grey."

The sentry knelt before her, his skin seeming a shade too green. Thea rubbed her eyes and blinked. The sentry stared back at her, his gaze dark and depthless. She wiped a palm over her leg, sliding it carefully up to her belt, but her blade was gone. The sentry smiled, showing a row of sharpened teeth, and his hands came up, his fingers lengthening into claws.

She opened her mouth to scream, but there was a sudden hollow *smack* as a bat landed solidly against the side of his head. The sentry—the *changeling*—slammed into the wall of the corridor, its body going limp for a moment before it bounded up, giggling, to race down the hall. Two actual sentries stared after it then drew their swords and gave chase.

Thea gaped down the corridor after them until Steed fell abruptly on top of her. She grunted and rolled him onto her lap. He gasped, pressing a hand to his chest. His other hand fell limply, and the busted wood of a table leg he'd used as a bat rolled free. She turned his head toward her as he took another breath. He held up a finger as if indicating he needed just a moment, and a cough wracked his chest. She winced, dabbing at the blood that trickled down his cheek. He would need stitches, but that would have to wait.

Thea passed him what was left of the water, and after a drink, she helped him to his feet. "Ready?"

He stared down at her, appearing about as unready as she felt, and drew a dagger from his belt. He pressed it into her palm, curling her fingers around it with his own. He held it there for a moment. He didn't speak, but she understood. She took a deep, steadying breath then followed Steed as they ran down the hall.

RUBY

Ruby screamed with every part of her being. Fire shot through her hands and over her skin, energy pulsing from her and into the beings who dragged her away. Venom pooled in her mouth as she twisted, biting hard through leather and flesh. It did no good. She was caught again, and it had not been a willing sentry who was dragged along with her. It was Grey, fighting and bleeding and drawn from his castle rooms, as she had been. He'd been ordered to protect her, to take down any fey who tried to reach Ruby ever again. He'd done that well enough, she guessed, as a half dozen of them had littered the dark stone floor. But they had been outnumbered, and the protections she'd set had been lost to spells stronger than hers.

Pitt had been coming for her all along, and she had known it, but it hadn't made a difference.

The spiders threw her onto the flat earth of a small clearing in Hollow Forest, an open space that had once been littered with stone but had turned to no more than dust, the keystones shattered in every part of the realm when Veil and

Pitt had faced off during the fates' dance. Some had thought the energy had destroyed the stones, others that they had been torn to dust when Pitt's magic was no longer holding them in place. Ruby knew better. Ruby understood that it had all been part of his plan.

Grey slammed to the earth beside her, his perfect face smacking the ground hard enough to draw blood. He pressed up with both hands, their healing flesh too pink in the late-day sun. He grabbed for his sword, which was missing, and then for the knives at his belt, stepping in front of Ruby before she even had a chance to find her feet.

She was so angry that she felt as if she could burn the very soul from that cursed changeling's body. She screamed again. It was a bit of a roar.

The changeling's laugh echoed through the clearing, and the haze of Ruby's fury cleared enough that she could take in their surroundings. They were centered in a ring of tall trees, the charred earth and broken limbs of their previous visit gone, swallowed by wild new growth. Their audience consisted of a smattering of changeling fey, tattooed spiders, and—horribly—Chevelle. He stood with his arms pinned behind him, staring beneath a lowered brow at Grey. She cursed her temper, because she'd clearly missed some unspoken communication between the two.

"How in the name of the plague did they get you?"

Chevelle let his level glare tip toward her. She winced. But he wasn't quite angry enough for something bad to have happened to Frey, so she let her gaze continue across the clearing, finding Pitt. He stood straight, his face flawless and his thin cloak unspoiled, and yet there was something off in the color of his skin.

She smiled. "Not quite yourself, I see. Seems a shame you've lost your ruby."

His answering smile was not nearly so mocking as her own—it held something more like a promise of pain. "I no longer need that stone." His words lingered in the air, stinging with the power that had spelled them to life. "Now, I have you."

Ruby resisted the urge to look back at Chevelle. Pitt had been bound from using magic and from spellcasting, and he'd still been able to spell his words into being. It did not bode well for their situation.

"You do not have me," she said coldly. "There is nothing on Earth that could bind me to your will."

Pitt allowed her to take in his smirk before letting his gaze roam over Grey.

"You might as well have done with me now," Ruby said. "Because you will get nothing of me ever again. Not after what your underlings did before. I will die first."

She said the words with all sincerity, but Ruby knew there was some purpose for his keeping them there. Pitt had been captured and bound. During the fates' dance ceremony, he had broken the highest of fey laws. If he risked staying in plain sight, there where the base energy ran so near the surface, he had sufficient reason for doing so. He was waiting for something.

Ruby drew the fire into her palms. Keane had been the most powerful fire fey on their lands. Pitt had not chosen to ally with him without cause. But Keane was dead, killed at the hands of another changeling fey, turned into ash and dust by Liana.

"You will die by my flame," Ruby promised him, "before the sun sets on fey lands."

Pitt's gaze flicked to the side, but before Ruby could act, spellwoven ropes were cutting against her limbs. She let loose her fire and Grey his blade, but there were too many forces working against them, and a moment later both she and Grey were caught in a web of spells and twine.

Pitt flicked a finger, and Ruby's bindings were yanked to the side, pulling her feet from beneath her so she landed hard onto the stone. He rolled his eyes at her resulting glare then walked gracelessly from the clearing as he uttered, "Bring them," to his men.

Ruby met Grey's gaze, certain her concern was evident and plain. The changeling fey was taking them farther into Hollow Forest. The sun was falling low, the night things taking flight.

In a matter of hours, the fires of Hollow Forest would seep through the broken earth to light a deadly game, and the changelings loved to play.

FREY

I STOOD BEFORE THE WOMAN I'D KNOWN FOR THE WHOLE OF MY life, even during the times I did not know my own self, and could only shake my head in disbelief. "Why are you telling me this now? Chevelle has been taken by a changeling fey in league with plague knows who else, the fey lord has disappeared after him, and I've got a menacing little changeling here trying to tell me what to do."

Junnie glanced over my shoulder at where Liana waited in what was left of the broken trees. Anvil stood beside her, weapons in hand, with Rhys and Rider farther out, unbearably still. *We do not have time for this.*

"The humans are not solely Pitt's responsibility." Junnie's voice was low, though I was fairly certain Liana and all of my guard could hear her. "Asher, too, had a plan to take control of them."

I frowned at her, not entirely surprised but not wanting to delve into it just then.

"He'd been planning it since the moment he ensnared my sister. He obtained her easily enough but not without cost.

And though she refused his bidding, she still possessed a special gift. She still held sway over animals." Junnie did not mention her sister's ability to sway humans, nor did she remind me that Asher had taken the child he'd created with her as well—my mother.

Thoughts of the massacre surfaced, of my mother in a rage, bringing in an army of men. It had been an attempt to stop him, as had Fannie's actions. Both had turned to an opportunity for the old Council, the Order of Light Elves—to overrun the North and cripple our rule. "And so… what? What does any of that matter now?" I had been restored to the throne. Junnie had taken headship of a new Council. All of it was over.

She cleared her throat. "I did not wish Isa removed from my side merely to keep you in your role as lord." She glanced again over my shoulder, but that time, I thought her eyes might have met those of the eldest and most brutish of my guard. "I needed her removed because she holds evidence that could damage far more than either of us or our new duties."

"Junnie," I whispered, "my Second waits for me at the hands of a deadly fey. If you cannot hurry this tale along and tell me what the curses you're talking about…"

The corner of her lips drew down. "Asher figured it out. Some sort of dark spellwork, worse than what he used to gather power. But all of it tied together, somehow, the energy within her and the talent she holds drawn from his castings."

My mouth went dry. Old secrets, dark and unspeakable things I'd hoped to never think of again, rose from the past. They crawled up my spine, raising the fine hairs of my neck and niggling at the back of my mind. It was bad. Worse than bad.

Junnie could see I understood. But she didn't know the half of it. "The safest place for Isa to be is on barren ground, where the fey cannot reach her without exhausting their power and where my own people cannot discover the darkness inside of her."

I wanted to ask her what this had to do with the fey, with Isa, with any of it. But I was afraid I knew. Asher had used the fey for his experiments—his children. He had made a deal with the fey. "What else?" I whispered.

She sighed. "He used the knowledge he'd gained to cast over Isa when she rested inside her human mother's womb." Junnie swallowed hard, as if remembering something horrible. "It was too late when I realized. The child had already come to term."

I bit back the curse that wanted to tear free of me. Junnie had kept it a secret since before Isa had been born. She had protected her ever since without a word of it to me. "Again, I ask, what importance does this have now, when my people are waiting in Hollow Forest?"

She straightened, apparently no longer interested in restraining her tone. "Asher made a deal with the changelings. But the fey were double-crossed and forced to gather the remaining knowledge themselves, so that they might protect themselves from the damage they'd all wrought."

The humans. The reason they'd taken Ruby. I felt the chill up my spine again, that darkness of times so far away. They'd not just taken Ruby—they'd taken her mother's diary—another fey who'd discovered the means to keep halfbreeds alive.

Asher had spelled my line's power over the humans into Isa, and in that regard, she was stronger than any of us. He'd told the changeling fey he could do the same, spell into them the ability Ruby had, so that they weren't tied to the base energy.

"But don't they understand?" I asked Junnie. "This isn't the same. Ruby can live free of the base magic because she's half elf. Because that part of her does not need to be tied to it."

"No," Junnie said. "She's able to harness it because she survived. Because she lives and is part of both and therefore can hold the energy of her fey blood along with the magic of our own."

I recalled long ago, when Junnie held the small babe in her hands. The human, Molly, had not survived childbirth, and Junnie had saved the infant, hidden her away. "Asher told the girl her babe would be king," Junnie had said, as if such a thing were true in a land of lords and councils. But he had never meant for her to be ruler of his own lands. He had far greater plans in place.

I didn't know whether he'd intended for his child to be a king of human lands or of a wider realm altogether. To each of his children, he'd promised a rule, and each of them had been built for a special kind of toil.

Junnie needed me to know that my predecessor had made a deal with the fey.

As we tore into the sky at the hands of flying fey, Liana's warning from long before echoed through my ears: "Do not chase after the halfling. She will have her own path. Save the others."

I trusted Liana not at all, but she had made bargains with my own allies even as her kind made them with the man who'd started the whole thing. I could not discount that she'd risked herself against Asher and Pitt's plans.

We dove through the trees of Hollow Forest, their jagged leaves cutting even at the fey. We slammed through them, crashing into the open air again only to hit a wall of scents that burned my nose. Sulfur and spice and strange flora were thick in every breath, but no trees or plants grew where the fires would burn. The ground was a dark mass of jutting rock, spiking skyward and diving to depths that left nothing for the eye but shadow and stone.

At the edge of that stone was the changeling, Pitt, a horde of his men, and Ruby, Grey, and Chevelle.

The fey carrying us took to ground at the edge of the trees near Pitt, and behind us, I heard the chattering and cheers of countless more fey, our audience.

My gaze found Chevelle where he stood bound, his arms behind his back and a line of blood smeared over the side of his face. I felt the tremor of magic rumble through me, but the cool touch of the staff held me from acting too rashly. I stared into his dark-blue eyes, so like the depths of a shadowed sapphire, like his mother's. That dark secret, one that only he and I knew, surfaced again, wanting to steal my focus. It was a secret that should never have reappeared, one that should have died with Asher.

But Asher had been consorting with fey. And there we were, dancing around a tale we'd vowed never to speak of about the dark magic Rune and Asher had played with and the other things no one else knew.

My fingers tightened on the grip of the staff. Asher and Rune had known what they were doing. Those sessions, the training, all of it had been a ruse. They'd been teasing out ways to spell the magic, searching for breaks in the surface to let themselves in. It had happened well before I came along, long before Isa.

It had just taken him so many years to perfect it that one of us had finally caught up with his deeds. I had taken him down before he could implement his plan.

"Release them now or suffer the consequences by my hand."

Pitt laughed, which could only be more insulting because he'd had to spell the sound to life. "And what would you do to me, Lord Freya, that has not already been warned?"

I smiled a wicked grin I'd learned in my youth. Asher had wanted me as his own. He had studied the boundaries the ancients had laid into place to discover how they affected fey magic. He had studied methods with which to transfer and bind. He had wanted me for my talent, to control an army of humans and bring down his enemies. He had wanted me at his side. He had used Chevelle to hurt me, had tried to turn me against my own mother.

Asher had taught me more than how to fight. He had taught me how to be cruel. He'd taught me how to win.

I lifted my staff a breath off the ground and let my smile fall away. When I slammed it again to the earth, it was without regard for the fey standing behind me or Junnie at my side. It was only for the changeling fey who threatened to destroy us, who aimed to bring down the very people from whom he had come.

Ruby's scream tore through the clearing, echoing off the jagged stone. Rock crumbled and shattered, falling with a scattering of trees into the pit below the formations of dark rock. My magic rolled through it, slamming into those on the other side. Chevelle knocked into Grey's side, forcing him to take a knee as Chevelle did, but Ruby was too far from them, tied and bound by spellwoven ropes, the ends of which rested in the changeling's hand.

Pitt's form shifted into something not quite elven, his shade going a sickly green, and beside me, despite the thundering rattle of earth, Junnie loosed an arrow. It stabbed into the changeling's hand, but he did not free Ruby. Pitt's fingers only shifted, sliding over the rope and back again, not letting her go. When the stone collapsing into the earth hit what lay beneath it, columns of flame shot toward the sky. Two of Pitt's fey were hit, the rest splitting to take hold of their prisoners or cover Pitt's back.

Anvil was running toward them with half of my guard, and Rhys and Rider had disappeared into the trees. A black wolf leapt from the dark forest, launching onto the back of the enemy fey, and he let loose a scream as the beast tore through the flesh of his shoulder, dragging him toward the ground where the wolf's brethren piled on.

The fey in the trees behind us shouted and cheered. They did not care who was lost as long as the base energy was fed, chaos reigned, and destruction was had. And there in the dark of Hollow Forest, mayhem was about to be unleashed.

My power rippled through the earth, delivering a continuous strike to the changeling fey. But he was not a weak being, and he had managed to break free of his bonds to reach the river of power beneath the fey lands. With Ruby at his side, he gritted his teeth in an ever-changing face and rolled into something new, something taller, thinner, not in the least alluring or pleasant, and a bit gray.

Ruby's face contorted in pain as she raised her eyes to the sky. Her mouth came open as if to scream, but instead, only fire burst from her form.

It was not the fire of a halfling girl. It was the fire of Hollow Forest. It was flames of an energy that did not feel wholly fey.

Junnie loosed another arrow, taking down one of Pitt's men. I could see her expression and knew that she was realizing what was happening along with me. Keane had been the most powerful fire fey. Pitt had used him, and now that he was gone, he planned to use Ruby instead, but Ruby was not a full-blooded fey. It would kill her.

I was running before good sense could get in the way. Across the broken earth, Rhys slammed his staff into one fey while Rider cut down another. Rider's sword swung perilously close to Chevelle and Grey, and then Chevelle stood, his hands finally free of the magic holding him. He did not glance at me as he moved for the changeling, and my feet moved faster still. Grey was headed for Ruby, her body alight with the flames of dark energy that rose from the earth. Grey was already burned, but it was no simple fire. One of Veil's fey slammed into one of Pitt's, the power of it crashing into the energy of the field.

Chevelle reached into a pouch at his hip, only strides away from the changeling fey, and one of Junnie's poisoned arrows struck Pitt in the neck. He growled, flashing a row of sharpened teeth, and snapped the wood to fall from his flesh. Grey reached Ruby with Rhys behind him, and the two threw up hands to attempt to douse the flame with magic.

Chevelle crashed into Pitt, knocking him backward, and the changeling wrapped his hands over Chevelle's neck, not to choke him but to reach bare skin, to better serve his power. Chevelle returned the favor, and the two locked in a physical battle just as I neared. I held the staff upward, and Anvil swung at the back of the changeling's knees. Anvil's sword sliced through flesh, cracking bone, just as Chevelle was hit with a blast of power that threw him across the field and nearly into the chasm of jagged rock.

I focused all my energy through the cold ironwood of my staff, and power exploded from its stone.

Pitt caught it, dragging me near, and between us struggled the energy of the base magic and every bit of power Asher had gathered with darkness and spellwork before he'd given it to me.

Energy seared through me, ice and fire in an unbearable storm, and I fought to gain control. Pitt's face had gone the color of earth and soil, and I could feel the flesh of my palm burning against the ironwood staff. I pressed it forward, focusing harder through its stone, and felt the tremor of a hairline crack splitting across its surface.

Something dark snaked up my legs, curling in wisps and semisolid claws. My stomach dropped. It was not the work of Chevelle, who had been knocked near the chasm of stone by the changeling. It was something else, someone with a talent for spellwork and dark magic.

The claws of smoke tightened around me, crawling slowly up my torso and onto my arms. I tried to shout for help, but my teeth were gritted hard against the effort to fight Pitt. Our power slammed and twisted, fighting against itself and roiling into a squall.

The spells rose higher, tugging at my arms, curling their fingers over the skin of my throat.

Someone else, my mind kept saying. *Something dark. Something that is going to cause us all to lose.*

Junnie's power slammed into Pitt, and Ruby's scream shifted into a weak and dying sound, not because less power ran through her but because it was more, too much for her to handle. I squeezed my damaged hand tighter around the staff, hurling every bit of my energy into the stone.

There was a moment of stillness—only the whisper of a breath—when my magic seemed as if it were taking the upper hand. It felt as if that one gem could focus my strength exactly where it needed to be and I could finally overcome the base energy and that single changeling fey.

Then the stone exploded.

FREY

THERE WAS A FLASH OF LIGHT AND THEN A SUDDEN, ALL-consuming darkness. I thought for a moment that I might have been blinded, but flickers of movement danced before my eyes. My body was wet and warm. Something solid pressed against my back in unsteady beats. My ears rang hollowly, and my mouth tasted of sulfur and something metallic.

My body jerked, and the pressing against my back became sharp and stinging. My hearing roared to life with the rush of the fight, with shouting and screaming and the crashing of trees. Something wrapped tightly around my leg, and I started, remembering the spells, but my vision cleared to find that I was hanging upside down, over a chasm.

I drew in a sharp, searing breath, and my body screamed in pain. The jagged rocks of the broken pit slammed into my shoulder, and as I flailed back to life, I became aware of frantic shouting. I stared up my own body to find the source of it: Junnie. She held tightly to my ankle, but I could see that her own injuries and the angle of my useless form were weighing her down.

Then I saw spikes of black creeping over her—the spellwork had hold of her shoulder and arm. Her expression said we'd only a matter of breaths. I glanced beneath me into the depths of the chasm and wished I hadn't. Far below was nothing but darkness. At my back was nothing but shards of stone. I tried to reach my power, but my body seemed broken. My hands were a mess of blood and torn flesh.

The fires above us lit the sky, but the flicker of flame was broken by a sudden shadow.

Veil's wide wings cut through the air as he dove down, grabbing hold of my torso to sling me toward Junnie. We crashed onto the ledge of the chasm, the spellwork surrounding her puffing into inky smoke before reforming. Veil was bloodied and snarling, and I had a feeling he must just have escaped from a trap of his own. He was free now, though, and he strode toward what I realized must have been the body of the changeling fey. I didn't have time to watch him because Junnie was gasping for air.

I pushed the edge of her cloak away, but the spell held fast. There was nothing I could do. I glanced up, frantic, to find Chevelle crawling toward us. He'd been hurt badly by his fight with the fey, but his hands were blackened, oily things, and I knew he'd done what he needed to help us end Pitt. I glanced again at Veil, who stood gloriously over a broken changeling, and could see that bit at least would soon be done. Chevelle reached Junnie's feet and threw ashen dust over the ground around us. It hissed and sizzled against the other spell, but Junnie still struggled for breath.

"What do I do?" My voice was raw, and all of me hurt, but the drive of the battle still roared through my veins.

Chevelle coughed then purposefully glanced across the

field. As he began muttering the words of a spell, I followed his gaze to find Ruby, who was still burning, swallowed by flame.

My eyes caught Chevelle's once more, and I knew that he had Junnie. It would take time, but he would save her. I leapt up, staggered, and fell forward. Anvil slammed into me, knocking me backward as he parried to save me from an oncoming blow. He shouted something, but Rhys had my arm and was dragging me away. I was unstable, but I could feel the magic inside me wanting to find its way out. Rhys propped me against him as we made our way across a battlefield of broken fey and shattered rock. A golden cloak from one of Junnie's personal guards lay bloodied and torn, and shards of steel were scattered over the ground.

Rhys came to a stop before the inferno that was Ruby, and we fell to our knees beneath the heat of her flame. Grey waited there with his hands against the stone and Rider beside him, as if in supplication. I followed suit, placing my blistered palms onto the cold, flat stone. Rhys's magic flowed through it already, and I could feel the cool burn of it as it joined his brother's. They were trying to douse the flame and counter the magic, but that was not how it would work. There was an endless supply.

"We need to tear her free," I said, "away from the fire and away from her tether to Pitt."

Grey stared up at me, his concern plainly on his face. It might kill her.

"If we wait, she may suffer the same fate." My words were cold but not untrue. With my head down once more, away from the searing heat, I prayed it would be neither and that we could save her.

Before my magic could be loosed into the earth, through

the stone and the source of the energy in the darkness below, a cool hand gripped my shoulder.

I glared up at Liana.

She did not bother to look at me when she spoke. "Either way will end her now. She's too far into the darkness to come safely free."

"We will not do nothing."

Liana had to have known that by then. She would have her own plan, and I wished she would just get on with telling us what it was. "There is a darkness beyond what lies beneath the Hollow Forest. You would do well to heed my warning."

"What would you have us do?"

She looked at me, her eyes a chasm of blackness. "The darkness must be doused, not the halfling. If it is done quickly, there is a chance I can save her."

My stomach dropped. "I can't. The energy here is too powerful to wield on my own."

"Not you," Liana said. "Only the fey lord can move the river of energy beneath the earth here."

I turned to find Veil and winced as he lifted the body of the changeling fey to tear it in two. He turned to face us, as if he'd heard Liana's words—but he would have, because she'd spelled them to life.

Liana was a changeling.

Veil strode toward us, not bothering to fly, and I became abruptly aware of our position on the stone, with our palms and knees to the earth in supplication.

I stood to face him. "We're out of time."

His gaze flicked to Liana then back to me. "Did she tell you it could kill me?"

I frowned. She had not mentioned that bit.

"Why would I risk that for some halfling girl?" Veil asked as I waited.

My mouth went dry, tasting of nothing but ash and copper. *This is it, then. He wants a bargain. I will have to sacrifice Ruby or—or what? What could he want? It doesn't matter. I won't do it.* I couldn't.

Beside me, a small breath escaped one of my Seven. I didn't have to look to know it was Grey. It was only the slightest sound, but I could feel every bit of pain behind it.

He was watching Ruby die.

I swallowed back the words that wanted to rise and glanced at Chevelle with Junnie. Every time we came onto fey lands, our lives were put in danger, but we could not stay secure in our castle—our home—because the darkness was spreading. It wasn't merely coming for the fey. It was coming for all of us.

"What do you want?" I said.

Veil stared at me incredulously. "My life," he snapped. "Do you expect to bargain with it again?"

"Pitt would have betrayed me, and you know it. I had no other choice."

His jaw went tight. "Your disloyalty to our agreement aside, you well know that I cannot risk my own skin when the entire realm is already in peril. Think of the chaos to follow."

"You think she isn't worth it," I told him, "but if you do not save her, we will walk away." My voice was steel, and in it was the threat of not just abandonment by my Seven and me, but by all of us, Junnie and Isa and the entire lot of his potential allies in the fight with the changelings against the darkness was coming.

Veil was unimpressed. "Do not threaten me, Lord Freya."

"I've barely even started."

Heat flared behind me, and Rhys and Rider shifted at my side. Their power was moving around us, fighting the inferno that I knew would take Ruby down. We were running out of time. I could not sacrifice my kingdom in an attempt to save her or throw away my own life when so many others depended on it. But I was asking—demanding—that the fey lord to do the same.

"Is she worth it to you?" His voice was low, curious. Saving his lands, Veil could understand, but risking all for a single halfling, not as much.

I took a long breath. "We love her." And then, because I doubted he would ever get that, I added, "She's part of who we are."

"And what for me?" he asked.

"A debt. Our gratitude."

"You will do whatever it takes to save our kind." His voice was level and clear, the words a bargain waiting to be sealed.

It was not to be taken lightly, but I would unquestionably do whatever it took to save an entire population from destruction. I could do nothing else. I released a slow breath, said my vow. "Whatever it takes."

There was a beat of silence, utter stillness, and then the smallest crook to the corner of Veil's mouth. I felt the blood drain from my face and turned to Liana.

Her expression was something short of a smile, her dark eyes rolling to meet mine. "It will be done."

And then she turned, raising her hands at her sides and melting into the blue-black of a raven's wing before shading to ash. Her power swelled through the stone, devouring the tingling of the others' magic and the heat of the fire. Veil moved beside her, his wings tucked tightly against his back and his fingers curled into claws. Together, they drew out the energy, bringing it from beneath the earth into a cloud of smoke and flame. Anvil was beside me, dragging me back from the storm and toward Chevelle. Junnie was coughing, her words too severed to make any sense. Chevelle's chants carried on, his voice hoarse and broken, but the smoke around Junnie appeared to be dissipating.

My eyes went back to Ruby, who was held taut in a vortex of darkness and fire. The energy Veil and Liana drew forth slowly swallowed up the flame. Ruby looked so small there, in the midst of it all, that I wondered how she could even be alive.

I leaned hard on Anvil, recalling that crook at the edge of the fey lord's lips. Stomach in knots, eyes running tears and ash, I choked out, "What have I done?"

Anvil squeezed me to him, his body so solid and strong that it was a comfort even covered in blood. "It is never what you have done," he told me quietly. "It is only what you will do."

FREY

RUBY LAY MOTIONLESS, THE RISE AND FALL OF HER CHEST imperceptible. We'd been assured it was there, even if my heart ached to see it. Liana's hands moved nimbly over Ruby, working to apply new tonics and herbs. She had sworn her stone on it, but I could not trust her after the bargain I'd just made.

I stared at Liana from the doorway. Her color had not returned, and I wondered what it had cost her to help save Ruby's life. Veil had paid a hefty price as well. They'd drawn the energy away from Ruby, and the ground had shaken as the earth around us crumbled into the darkness below Hollow Forest. It was nothing but a pit, the tendrils of rock and earth snaking their way from where the fey lord had stood all that kept us from falling within.

Veil had collapsed. He'd been lifted from the spot where he'd landed—from where he'd caught Ruby's limp body, so small and broken—and was carried through the sky to what I had assumed would be his home. But Veil's home was gone, all of it destroyed.

I felt no empathy, though, because all I saw when I thought of him was the tilt of his mouth. The crook of his lips had said he'd won.

That didn't matter anymore. Ruby was alive and would become well.

Pitt was dead. If Chevelle hadn't risked his own life to lay spelled hands on the changeling, he would have been able to draw that power through Ruby and the river beneath Hollow Forest. It could have devoured us all. Chevelle had saved us. Pitt was truly gone this time and no longer a threat.

But someone else had been there in the forest, as well, a powerful spellcaster capable of whatever plans the changeling had laid in place. Someone who would have been able to tie the thing that was part of how Ruby's magic worked to other fey and to release them from their bonds to the energy beneath the earth.

For too long, there had been far more at play than I'd been aware of. Before I'd even been brought into being, Asher had made plans with the fey. The changelings were not the only ones in on the plot, and my people were at risk before any of us had even known it. And I'd made another bargain with a fey lord.

We had been spared, but none of it was over. Not even close. I thought of Junnie and her confessions about Isa. Even she had known there was more to all of this. I could not help but wonder why everyone had held the secrets so close to their chests.

Chevelle had saved Junnie as well. The two did not agree on most things, but they'd formed a tenuous accord over restoring me. Junnie's men had taken her home, but she couldn't have been pleased that a spell had nearly brought her down. There would be recompense for whoever had done so.

The magic used for spellwork was a dark, malevolent

thing, and the one we had just defeated was especially vile. But Chevelle had the connection to the darkness required for casting. It was only that connection that allowed Junnie to live and breathe. Junnie's connection was only to the light magic, but mine was to both the light and the dark, and Veil's was to the fey energy.

"You should rest," Chevelle said beside me, sliding a hand over the small of my back.

I might have startled if I'd not been so exhausted. I frowned. "Pitt must have been in league with someone else, someone who had a connection—" I cut my words cut off when I realized Liana was still in earshot. I glanced at Chevelle. "The ability to spellcast at that level. Otherwise, he would not have been able to break the bonds you placed on him or to plan to cast whatever is necessary to bypass the base energy and sustain their own power."

He only watched me. He had worked it all out already, likely the first time the darkness had brushed his skin. But I couldn't trust any of the assumptions I'd always made. I couldn't help but wonder whether the deadening of the base energy was not the humans' fault at all and if the meddling with the darkness the fey and Asher had done had set it afoot to begin with. A chill ran over me at the memory of the dark magic and how it had always seeped through at Hollow Forest, exploding occasionally into fires. And now, Hollow Forest was gone. The darkness ran free.

"Come," Chevelle said. "There will be time enough to deal with what remains." I stared up at him, aware of the helplessness plain on my face. He gave me a smile, though the cut on his lip had to have made it painful. "What was it you promised me? The kingdom has your days."

But you have my nights. I let out a tired sigh and leaned into him. "Then let it be. For I am a woman of my word."

THEA

THEA WALKED THROUGH THE DARKENED CORRIDORS OF THE castle, the restrictions placed on the rest of the guard lifted from her. She was a healer, the only one they trusted to watch a changeling fey. Lord Freya had placed constant guards on Liana, but Thea was to drop in at least twice a day to check the herbs and poultices and to be certain Liana was not sneaking something unacceptable in.

Ruby had been returned to her rooms. She was far improved and occasionally awake, but the trauma she'd been through had not been easy on her, and it would be a while before she was recovered. It was better that way, because when she did come out of her stupor, she was notoriously hard to treat. When she wasn't smacking away Liana's ministrations, she was muttering nonsense about winged horses and flying elves.

The mess the fey had left behind was long gone, cleaned by the castle staff. Thea wasn't certain if the bodies had been burned, for when the fey died on elven lands, their magic could not be returned to the earth. She'd not asked, because her thoughts had been otherwise occupied in the week since the attack.

Things were settled again, though, and as she walked from the corridor into a stone courtyard, she felt the reassuring usualness of it all. Duer was working with a few of the newer recruits, their weapons sharp and deadly. A group of older guards stood nearby, watching a sparring match with longsword and spear. By the far wall was the dark-haired girl Thea had encountered in the dying lands past the fey forests, the one who had been helping Ruby. She was on her hands and knees, scouring the blocks with a well-worn brush. Barris stood over her, probably offering his aid, but the girl steadfastly refused. "I am of the guard," she snapped. "It is my duty."

Barris looked up at Thea, shaking his head. Thea bit back her smile, and Barris raised his shoulders in a shrug. There was really only so much he could do.

Thea walked through a tall stone archway, following the narrowing path ahead. She had finally found her nooks and crannies and could be counted on to hide in them at least once a day. The path wound farther from the interior of the castle, the structure's overhead stonework throwing light and shadow across her way. Before it reached the haven that was the stables, Thea ducked into an alcove, completely shadowed from the waning day.

The cool stone pressed against her back, and she took a slow, mind-easing breath. It could be so quiet in the darkness, so much more like the days she'd spent at home. Those times had been fraught with worry for her father, though, and that was all gone. When she searched out that stillness those days, it was only to find some peace, some small corner of her own, where she was not a guard to the North and its lord with the responsibilities that entailed but where she was only Thea.

A shadow shifted in the cool quiet of her darkness, but

Thea did not flinch. There was something in it that was slow, smooth, and familiar. "Have you never been warned away from lurking in the shadows?" Her hand rested on the hilt of her dagger, evidence she was not to be trifled with.

Light caught on Steed's careful smile as he moved closer then disappeared as he came closer still.

They had spoken since their disagreement in the courtyard, though not about anything other than the fey attack and their castle duties. They'd had to heal after the battle and the poison, and they'd had no chance to be alone.

A strange sensation tingled through Thea's fingers. They were alone now.

Steed came to rest a breath before her, so close that she had to curl her hands into fists to keep from reaching out. It was dark there, but her eyes had adjusted. She could see the way he looked down at her. She remembered what she'd said to him, that she was not what he wanted, that she was not enough. She'd been taunting him, intending to put him through the wringer until the ideas had gone from his head. She'd not meant to leave the words the way she had.

Her throat went dry, but it was far too late to take it back. Steed had been simmering for a week. From the looks of things, he had every intention of setting her to rights.

He leaned in closer, his expression solemn. He took one of her hands in his, leaving her other to clutch lamely at her dagger. "You think that I am not certain." His voice was low, and in the nearness of the alcove, it seemed to rumble through her like a vow. Steed's gaze cut into hers, holding her very, very still. "But more than anything else, I am certain… of you."

Thea swallowed hard, willing her voice not to tremble, her smile not to betray the way the words cut to her heart. "And just how do you intend to keep me happy? By being reliably steady and patient, the way you've always been with your stock?"

His smile tipped up at the edge. He murmured, "And keeping treats in my pocket if I need to."

Thea laughed, and he let her, watching the way it transformed her face. She didn't think she would ever get tired watching him waiting for her smile or of how his attention could focus solely on her.

"Is that agreeable to you?" he asked.

Thea's smile fell, and she promised, "I can't imagine anything more agreeable."

He leaned down, the two of them entirely alone in the shadow of the alcove, and pressed his lips to hers.

Thank you for reading. Please look for book six in the Frey Saga: *Feather and Bone*

THE FREY SAGA

Frey

Pieces of Eight

Molly (a short story)

Rise of the Seven

Venom and Steel

Shadow and Stone

Feather and Bone

DESCENDANTS SERIES

Bound by Prophecy

Shifting Fate

Reign of Shadows

SHATTERED REALMS

King of Ash and Bone

Queen of Iron and Blood

HAVENWOOD FALLS

Toil and Trouble

BAD MEDICINE

Blood & Brute & Ginger Root

∼

Visit the author on the web at

www.melissa-wright.com

www.ingramcontent.com/pod-product-compliance
Lightning Source LLC
Chambersburg PA
CBHW070942190726
48292CB00004B/1298